WALK YOU THERE

BOOKS BY JAN THOMPSON

CITY/COASTAL/BEACH ROMANCE

Seaside Chapel (7 Books)

JanThompson.com/seaside

Savannah Sweethearts (12 Books)

JanThompson.com/savannah

Vacation Sweethearts (8 Books)

JanThompson.com/vacation

ROMANTIC SUSPENSE/THRILLERS

Protector Sweethearts (6 Books)

JanThompson.com/protector

Defender Sweethearts (6 Books)

JanThompson.com/defender

Binary Hackers (4 Books)

JanThompson.com/binary

JanThompson.com/books

WALK YOU THERE

SAVANNAH SWEETHEARTS
BOOK SIX

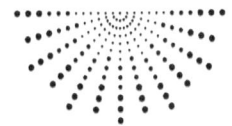

JAN THOMPSON

GEORGIA
PRESS

WALK YOU THERE (SAVANNAH
SWEETHEARTS BOOK 6)

Copyright © 2016 Jan Edttii Lim Thompson

Published by Georgia Press LLC
Author Website: JanThompson.com
Book List: JanThompson.com/books
Book News: JanThompson.com/newsletter

The Savannah College of Art and Design (SCAD) is mentioned
with permission from the university.

eBook Cover Design: Georgia Press LLC
Paperback Cover Design: Georgia Press and Deranged Doctor
Design

eBook ISBN 978-1-944188-05-4
Paperback ISBN 978-1-944188-30-6

To my Lord and Savior, Jesus Christ, who died on the cross to save me from my sins and rose again from the grave to give me eternal life in heaven.

For God so loved the world that He gave His only begotten Son, that whoever believes in Him should not perish but have everlasting life.
—John 3:16

READ A FREE EBOOK IN THE
SAME STORY WORLD

Set in Georgia, South Carolina, and Tennessee, this clean and wholesome Christian romance tells the story of art gallery archivist Sheryl Breckenridge and world-famous sculptor Winton Pace. Read this ebook for free!

Time for Me (A Vacation Sweethearts Prequel)
JanThompson.com/time-free

ABOUT THE SAVANNAH SWEETHEARTS SERIES

Welcome to the new south! From *USA Today* bestselling author Jan Thompson come these clean and wholesome, sweet and inspirational Christian romances set in the coastal city of Savannah, Georgia, and on the beaches of Tybee Island by the Atlantic Ocean.

Meet a group of multiracial and multiethnic churchgoing Christians who love the Lord, work hard in their careers, and seek God's will for their love lives. Against a backdrop of ocean, sand, and sun, these inspirational romances showcase aspects of the human need for God and for one another.

Have some tea, settle in a comfortable reading chair, and enjoy these sweet celebrations of faith, hope, and love in Jesus Christ.

SAVANNAH SWEETHEARTS

- Book 1: Ask You Later
- Book 2: Know You More
- Book 3: Tell You Soon
- Book 4: Draw You Near
- Book 5: Cherish You So
- Book 6: Walk You There
- Book 7: Love You Always
- Book 8: Kiss You Now
- Book 9: Find You Again
- Book 10: Wish You Joy
- Book 11: Call You Home
- Book 12: Let You Go

While Savannah Sweethearts books can be read as standalone stories, you can see a bigger picture of the Riverside Chapel community and get a glimpse of the futures of previous characters if you read Books 1-12 in order.

SAVANNAH SWEETHEARTS BOOK 6

She wants to save history.
He wants to raze it all.

A local tour guide who makes a living off Savannah history goes to battle against an award-winning developer who wants to demolish the old city block she lives on.

TAMSYN'S TROUBLES...

Tamsyn Pendegrast's troubles can be summed up in one word: Ryan.

Okay, three words: Ryan Ruttledge V.

A nightmare to her historical preservation

efforts, an enemy of her fledgling Tamsyn Tours travel agency and tour company, Ryan seems to have it all: funding, support, awards, and the deeds to half the properties on Rosa Pendegrast Lane in old-town Savannah. Only three historic homes remain unsold. One of them is the Pendegrast family home where Tamsyn has lived since she was a baby.

Savannah residents will not take this destruction sitting down. Tamsyn is sure of it. No way will they let Ruttledge Yamada Urquhart Commercial Properties turn her nineteenth-century city block into a ghastly sprawl of glass-and-steel sculpture. It's Tamsyn's duty to Savannah history and to the memory of the Pendegrast family to educate that Ryan dude on why he should just leave the past alone.

There. Her task is set.

If only he wasn't so charming...

RYAN'S RUCKUS...

Three more houses to buy, and the city block will belong to Ryan's commercial property company. Then he will reshape the area into a modernist architectural creation. One more award to win, and one more plaque to hang on the wall of his Atlanta office. Easy peasy, right?

All he has to do is get past Tamsyn Pendegrast.

That small-town tour guide has a property he wants. One house. How hard can it be to get one house? If she sells her ramshackle old house, her two neighbors will follow.

Why is she holding out? His company has offered Tamsyn three times the value of her property. That worn and weary Queen Anne style Victorian house isn't going to last through the twenty-first century, anyway. Its foundation has been reinforced twice, and no amount of paint will restore it to its old glory. Tamsyn is simply holding on to a past that cannot be regained. She might as well give it up.

And yet, Tamsyn's tenacity intrigues him. It's messing with his mind.

And heart.

Uh-oh.

Walk You There (Savannah Sweethearts Book 6)
JanThompson.com/walk

Savannah Sweethearts
JanThompson.com/savannah

Jan Thompson's Book News Mailing List:
JanThompson.com/newsletter

WALK YOU THERE

CHAPTER ONE

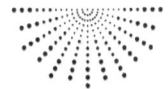

"*T*amsyn Tours. How may I help you?"

The sweet, euphonious voice filled Ryan Ruttledge's ears. He blinked. His talking points were at the tip of his tongue, but now they had vaporized.

What did I say her voice was?

"Hello?"

"Um... Is that Tamsyn Pendegrast?" Ryan asked. *Um?* Was that the best he could do?

Silence.

"This is Ryan Ruttledge. May I speak with Tamsyn?"

More silence.

"Hello?" Ryan tried again.

Click.

Actually, it sounded more like someone had just

thrown her cell phone across the room, but then again, that couldn't possibly be the case since the Tamsyn he had interacted with via emails, phone calls, and videoconferences the previous few months seemed to have a sweet, smiling nature—except when he had infuriated her.

Which had been about once in every conversation.

More so in the two weeks since Ruttledge Yamada Urquhart Commercial Properties had purchased half the rundown city block where Tamsyn lived in old-town Savannah.

On the phone a minute before, she had seemed to be back to her sweet self before she found out it was him on the other end of the line. He had his caller ID blocked, but the moment he had spoken, she had reacted.

Until then, her voice had been soothing to hear.

Euphonious—

Uh, did I say euphonious?

Ryan frowned. He couldn't remember the last time he used that word to describe a woman's voice on the phone.

He growled. "No one hangs up on Ryan Ruttledge V."

Across the room, between two large display tables featuring the talents of RYUCP, his business partner laughed like a hyena.

"Not helping, Hiroki." Ryan sank into his two-thousand-dollar task chair. He crossed his feet at the edge of the table.

"Last I checked, plenty of women hung up on Ryan Ruttledge V," Hiroki continued.

"Not when I'm offering them a sweet deal."

"Sweet? You want to raze her precious city block down to the ground and build a glass tower. That's not sweet to some people."

"It's a great deal. It'll revitalize that entire area," Ryan reasoned, almost to himself, but more so as a rehearsal to present to the people of Savannah. "I want that city block."

"She's in the way."

"She and that Save Old Savannah group of theirs. Who funds them anyway?" Ryan crossed the plush carpet to his cappuccino machine.

Hiroki Yamada was on it, swiping here and there on his iPad. "Mostly they themselves and local residents, perhaps. No famous families listed—wait! I spoke too soon. Here are a couple. Cavanaugh. Matheson. Old money."

"I'm not familiar with those names," Ryan said. "What about her own family? What are we up against?"

"Pendegrast? Not much information about them. We do know that Jerome Pendegrast owns two riverboats. He donated one to a church a while back."

"Riverside Chapel or something." Ryan made himself a small cup of hot cappuccino. "Want a cup?"

"Nope. Had too much today." Hiroki grinned. "Wouldn't Satan revel in the day that two Christians fight each other to the death over a bunch of dilapidated nineteenth-century buildings."

Ryan bristled. "Tamsyn and I are not *fighting* per se. We just have a disagreement—uh, many disagreements."

He was lifting the cup to his lips when it came loose from his fingers. The hot liquid splashed on his hand. He yowled.

Now there was a dark, hot mess on the camel-colored carpet in the open office.

Hiroki was on it with gobs of paper napkins.

"No, no." Ryan told him to get up. "My mess, my cleanup. Go compile the lowdown on the Pendegrast family. Something I can use to get Tamsyn on my side. She's the only one standing between me and our next architectural award."

"Just so you know, I've never been one for awards," Hiroki said.

"I know. You love the work. The work is its own reward, blah, blah."

Hiroki handed Ryan more paper napkins and

walked back to his workstation in the big room. "Do you want me to call housekeeping?"

"Later. I don't want them in here right now while I'm plotting the demise of Tamsyn Tours." Ryan dabbed the carpet. The patches of spilled coffee were still somewhat dark.

He made himself a fresh cup of cappuccino.

"How hard can it be?" Ryan asked no one. "They're just a bunch of no-name tour guides."

"Tour guides with backing from the Savannah people and some well-to-do families," Hiroki reminded him. "Old money dating all the way back to Charleston, in the days when it was known as Charles Towne."

"Was it?" Ryan sat down, savoring his caffeine. He had flunked American history in college but managed to pass the third time he had taken the class. It had helped that he had an easygoing teacher in the summer.

Hiroki nodded. "Don't mess with old money, is all I can say. They have staying power."

"Money can run out."

"That too."

"Seriously, she can't be that hard to knock down." Ryan logged into his laptop and browsed through the Tamsyn Tours website. "She's a small fry."

"Why did you say that?"

"She answered her own phone. Control freak."

"How do you know she's a control freak?" Hiroki asked. "Have you ever met her?"

"No, but all those videoconferences—"

"They mean nothing. You need to meet her in person."

"But all signs point to that. Her pretty voice, the way she sounds so pleasant on the speakerphone. All for show."

"You don't believe that."

Sweet.

Euphonious.

Noooo... I will not fall for that.

Hiroki spun around in his task chair. "There's only one thing to do, Ryan, old friend."

"What?" At this point, Ryan was out of options.

"You have to take a vacation in Savannah."

"Whatever for? I can buy that city block from here."

"But in your ivory tower, you can't see what the little people want."

Little people?

"The peasants." Ryan began to get it.

"When you're on the ground, you can find out what the fuss is about. You know, why she's been hating you for the last two months or more."

"Might be something I said."

"You think?"

Ryan brushed him off. He warmed up to the idea of a vacation on the coast of Georgia. It was April, and the weather would be nice. He could take a walk among the azaleas and get some photographs of those flowers his mother loved.

He had been so busy lately that he hadn't gotten back to his photography hobby. With Savannah's collection of architecture, there should be plenty of buildings to photograph and to identify for a buyout.

It would be a change of scenery for him from this landlocked Buckhead office.

Ryan sighed. "I hate that woman."

"But you'd love to have that corner property," Hiroki countered.

"Yeah. You'd think by the way she's taking this so personally that she's protecting her family farm."

"She is. That house has been in her family since the late nineteenth century. The road was renamed after her great-grandmother, remember?"

Rosa Pendegrast Lane.

"She's not going to give it up," Ryan concluded.

"Conceding already?" Hiroki laughed. "Face her like a man, Ryan."

"What did you say?"

"You heard me. We've been business partners for a long time, and you know I speak the truth." Hiroki waved his iPad in Ryan's face. "There's a public meeting tonight at seven o'clock at the river-boat. Just be sure to go to the right riverboat. Not Riverside Chapel. The other one. It's called—"

"I have to work tomorrow."

"I'll cover for you. Nothing happens on Fridays around here anyway. Take a long weekend off."

"You think I should attend the meeting," Ryan said.

"Especially when one meme she posted to social media says, 'Stand Up Against Ruttledge Yamada Urquhart, Savannah History's Nightmare.'"

"It says that? Let me see." Ryan motioned for Hiroki to hand him his iPad.

"Ah, she's taking it personally." The other memes in the series said worse things about Ryan. "I could sue her for defamation."

"One block of ramshackle buildings," Hiroki said, refocusing Ryan's thoughts.

Ryan nodded. "Yeah. How hard can it be to knock them down?"

How hard can it be to get past sweet Tamsyn?

Sweet?

Did I say sweet?

What's wrong with me?

CHAPTER TWO

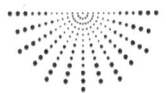

"What's wrong with him?" Tamsyn Pendegrast asked aloud as she stacked up her handouts on one of the tables in the upper deck dining room of the *Caleigh Pendegrast* riverboat.

There was supposed to be a chartered cruise tonight, but the clients had canceled it, and since nothing else was scheduled on board the riverboat this evening, Dad had let Tamsyn hold her meeting there.

The dining room was surrounded by a wide swath of windows. Outside, the city lights of Savannah sparkled in the wispy April evening all the way to a brightly lit Talmadge Memorial Bridge.

There was no rain tonight, and Tamsyn hoped for a big turnout.

It was an important event.

Hopefully not to only me...

Her friend, Heidi Wei-Flores, smiled. "Education, Tam, will bring him around."

"We say that because we were both history majors way back when, but that guy flunked American history in high school and in college." Tamsyn shuffled through her notes, highlighting her talking points.

"How did you know that?"

"Ming, who else?" Tamsyn glanced at the clock at the back of the dining room. If anyone had asked, she wouldn't admit she was anxious, but God knew she was.

"You asked my brother to look him up?" Heidi slid onto the seat next to her. Against her back, the second-floor dining room windows reflected the Savannah riverfront heading toward sunset.

"Yeah. All Ming wanted was my famous turkey chili."

Heidi laughed. "No wonder my brother's PI company isn't going anywhere. I don't know how he keeps getting paid in food, and not cash."

"Well, he has plenty of business elsewhere."

"True."

"And I told him I'd put the Savannah River Investigations logo on my company promotional materials for the next six months."

"Clever." Heidi shifted in her seat. "About this Ryan dude, what else did my brother find out for you?"

"That's all I got for a discount. I googled the rest." Tamsyn had committed it all to memory. "He only designs sleek, futuristic, steel-and-glass office complexes, from that award-winning three-hundred-floor tower in Dubai to the two-hundred-acre corporate headquarters for the Hot Dupree sauce company in Louisiana. He doesn't design anything that looks like the past or has any historical meaning."

Tamsyn stared at the wall clock. The meeting had been rescheduled to 7:30 p.m. It was almost time, and yet she and Heidi were the only ones there.

Had she lost the battle before she had begun?

Tamsyn blinked away a speck—or something—from her eyes.

Where were all her other tour guide friends? They had indicated they would come. But a Thursday night was not the best time to schedule an emergency meeting. It was April, after all, a busy season for garden and candlelight tours, both day and evening.

Of all the times of the year, Ryan Ruttledge had to pick a fight with her in the spring. At least it wasn't the summer, when tourism peaked in Savannah.

Yet never one to shrink from a fight, Tamsyn was ready to take him down.

If only the entire city of Savannah were with her.

As long as Rosa Pendegrast Lane remained a favorite venue of vandalism and an avenue of unoccupied buildings, there was little hope for her to keep her family home unless she had an infusion of cash.

Maintenance was key, but it was too late for some of those buildings.

However, if she could persuade the owners of the two other unsold homes to hold on to their properties, they might have some traction.

"Why doesn't the city stop him?" Tamsyn's frustration rose. "All they have to do is tell him no, and the entire block is saved from destruction."

"Money, Tam. Money," Heidi said.

"And the city thinks that Rosa Pendegrast Lane is a blight to its reputation." Tamsyn jostled the keys out of her purse.

"Having the highest rate of vandalism in Savannah doesn't help."

"That's a law enforcement problem, Heidi."

Tamsyn walked toward the old wooden double doors to the dining room. She unlocked the doors with care, as if the bolt and lock would fall right off if she used force. It was, after all, an old riverboat.

Dad had been loath to part with it because he had met Mom here. She had passed away some eight years before, but Dad was still grieving. Living on the riverboat was his way of dealing with his loss, Tamsyn supposed, but how long was he going to live there? He had donated the other riverboat to Riverside Chapel.

Tamsyn had invited Dad to move back into their family home on Rosa Pendegrast Lane, but he had refused. He had a point. Mom's signature was everywhere in that house.

She wondered if Dad would show up tonight. He had told her that she was fighting a lost cause but that he would stand with her.

Those old homes on Rosa Pendegrast Lane were as good as razed. Some called them charming, and some called them an eyesore.

It's history to me.

Heidi shook her head. "Sometimes I wonder if it's safe for *you* to live there."

"I lock my doors." She remembered when the area around her family home hadn't been this bad, but the economic slump in the previous decade hadn't left her neighborhood.

"That's not enough."

Tamsyn knew Heidi was right, but she'd think

about that later. She had grown up with the people in the area, and they knew one another. They wouldn't hurt her.

"My neighbors aren't the problem. Ryan Ruttledge is." Tamsyn opened the doors, breathed in the Savannah River air, and expelled a big sigh. "Seriously, what's wrong with him?"

Stomping shoes coming up the ramp connecting the riverboat to the Savannah waterfront stopped Tamsyn from complaining further.

Complain? Did I?

Several tour operators greeted Tamsyn, grabbed the evening's program from a nearby table, and took their seats.

Tamsyn swiped her iPad to check off the attendees. Dad should be coming up soon from his cabin downstairs.

She checked her email. A quick note from Piper Peyton said she couldn't make it tonight. Busy evening at the café.

Nadine Saylor couldn't make it either. She had to work as well.

Someone else walked in. And then another. Citizens. Business owners. Tour guides. Local historians with vested interest in the nonprofit organization that Tamsyn and Heidi had formed.

For Save Old Savannah to survive and to be taken seriously by the city, they needed more diversified support than local philanthropists and twenty members.

"I don't know how we're going to win this," one of the tour guides said.

"Tamsyn could write a book about Rosa Pendegrast," another said. "When are you going to finish that book, Tam?"

"Working on it," Tamsyn replied from where she was standing at the door. Sure, she had been working on that book for years. Never mind that she hadn't gotten past chapter two.

"Have you met this Ryan Ruttledge?" someone else asked.

"The fifth!" a booming voice added.

Dad!

Somehow, Tamsyn's spirit lifted. She was glad Dad had chosen her meeting over his TV shows.

"The fifth, I say." Dad stepped into the dining room. "Ryan Ruttledge V."

"I haven't met him in person," Tamsyn explained. "But we've videoconferenced and talked on the phone."

Their last encounter had been this morning when she hung up on him. She hadn't stuck around to find out why he had called.

"I saw him in the news," Heidi said. "He's kinda cute."

"The pit bull?" Tamsyn walked toward the crowd. "Cute?"

An unexpected male guffaw followed her.

"I've been called many things, but never a cute pit bull."

Tamsyn froze at the voice.

She turned around slowly and came face to face with none other than Ryan Ruttledge V. He was only several inches taller than she was, which meant he was about six feet to her five nine.

He looked different in person from those video-conference calls. Out of his usual oxford shirt and tie, in a plaid button-down and rolled-up sleeves, and with his brown hair tousled, why, he looked rather—

Attractive?

Eeeeeek...

"Should I trademark it?" Ryan continued.

"Trademark what?" Tamsyn tried to remain calm. *Remember that he is the enemy.*

The enemy!

"The Cute Pit Bull."

Tamsyn didn't smile. "If you're looking for the comic relief meeting, this is not it. We're serious here. We're trying to save old Savannah from history haters like yourself."

"I don't hate history. I love making it."

Tamsyn rolled her eyes. "Why destroy Rosa Pendegrast Lane?"

"Destroy? On the contrary, we're here to revitalize it. I'm sure many tour companies would love to showcase something new in Savannah. It'll help the economy."

"Is profit margin all you look at?" Tamsyn fumed.

Ryan stepped closer. "Got you angry, didn't I? Who's the Cute Pit Bull now?"

CHAPTER THREE

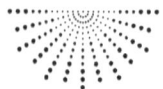

"That went well last night." Ryan Ruttledge crawled out of the king-sized bed as he recalled the Save Old Savannah meeting. It was still fresh on his mind even though he had slept in until nine o'clock this morning.

While the public had been welcomed to that meeting, it was clear he was not. Tamsyn had made a point not to answer his questions, not to get into a verbal fisticuff with him, not to make any eye contact with him throughout the one-hour meeting.

All Ryan wanted to do was help Savannah.

Truly.

If it meant adding a spark of interest into that dumpy corner of the city, then someone had to do it. It might as well be RYUCP with its award-winning architectural designs.

In the shower, Ryan made plans to show Tamsyn some of his favorite architectural designs around the world. RYUCP had been busy in Europe of late, designing gravity-defying glass towers.

Perhaps Tamsyn would be impressed when she saw how he had incorporated rooftop gardens into some of those multiuse complexes.

Everyone loves green designs these days.

Perhaps he could persuade her.

Perhaps not.

Fifteen minutes later, he was standing outside the hotel facing two-way traffic and pedestrians out and about. Tourists, probably.

The concierge had suggested a few places on River Street, including one he repeated twice: Piper's Place. But his hotel was far away from the Savannah River, and he didn't want to drive his rental car and look for a parking spot.

Technically, he could walk, but he felt lazy this morning.

Ryan decided to go four blocks down to the City Market where, supposedly, there were breakfast places. It turned out that the blocks were Savannah squares, covered with old trees and monuments.

His iPhone map took him down Barnard Street, which went around Ellis Square. He stopped at the square, took some photos on his iPhone, marveling at the old oak trees—live oak, they'd called them—all around him.

They must've taken hundreds of years to get that tall.

Surrounded by such an exhibition of old things, Ryan began to wonder about the history of the city. History had never been his strongest subject in school.

Although he had been born in North Carolina, he had grown up an Army brat, traveling the world, never calling a place home until he worked his way up in the architectural world.

Eventually, he started a commercial property business with Hiroki Yamada and Jared Urquhart. While RYUCP was one of the many companies that the Urquhart family had invested in, it was Ryan's only business, his bread and butter, as it was for Hiroki.

Ryan's entire career and reputation rested on the premise that he would continue to create and build award-winning buildings. The last thing he needed right now was to have some small-town tour operator squash his next conquest.

Rosa Pendegrast Lane is mine.

Ryan quickened his pace down Barnard, crossing the street to the City Market.

A trolley passed within inches of him, and came to a halt. Ryan hadn't realized he was walking that close to the edge of the sidewalk. He looked up, and the trolley said *Tamsyn Tours* on the side.

Through the open windows, Ryan heard her voice.

That euphonious voice.

"Here's the City Market. Tonight a local band is playing jazz and some blues. If you look outside, they're setting up the open area for some water-color exhibits. A local artist friend of mine, Abilene Dupree, has some paintings she'll be selling. Twenty percent off if you mention Tamsyn Tours."

Ryan stretched his neck. A tricorn hat was moving back and forth toward the front of the trolley. Underneath the hat was a mop of light-brown hair.

Tamsyn.

She happened to turn his way as she pointed out this and that in the City Market. Ryan couldn't help listening. It turned out that he was standing in one of the most historic places in Savannah.

Did it mean anything?

Ryan looked down on the ground. It was concrete like any other sidewalk.

But what's underneath?

What was once here?

Ryan looked back at the trolley, wondering what he should do. Wave to Tamsyn? Smile? Do nothing?

Before he could decide, the trolley moved on. Somehow Ryan felt a sense of loss.

Odd. Very odd.

That feeling remained with him as he found his way through the City Market, heading for a southern café open for breakfast.

While waiting for his eggs, ham, and grits, Ryan drank coffee and texted Hiroki.

Hiroki called him almost instantly.

"Any advice for me?" Ryan leaned back as his breakfast arrived.

"Take a tour. Be sure it's Tamsyn Tours."

"I thought of that and ruled it out."

"Why?"

"She hates me."

"Business is business. She's not going to turn away a tourist."

"You don't know her, Hiroki."

"Neither do you."

"Right. Let me think about it."

"Think fast. The next tour is in thirty-five minutes. Historic Homes. Your territory!"

Territory? "Ha! I wish. Somehow I have a feeling it's going to be an uphill climb to get past Tamsyn."

The Cute Pit Bull.

How endearing.

CHAPTER FOUR

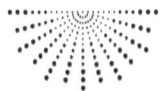

hat is he doing here?

Tamsyn tried to be nonchalant, but it irked her that Ryan Ruttledge had entered her world uninvited. She doubted he was standing in line now to board the trolley for the five-block walking tour because he was interested in the colonial history of Savannah.

Nope!

She was sure that he was there to spy on her, to find her weakness, and then to pounce on her and take away Rosa Pendegrast Lane.

He's a destroyer, not a preservationist.

Tamsyn kept telling herself that as she tapped her iPad to check off the list of customers for this walking tour. It wasn't strenuous to cover five city blocks, and most anyone could do it, even in a wheelchair.

Still, the crowd was thin today, and that bothered her too.

She usually led about twelve or fifteen customers at most, and her other tour guides would take another ten or twenty. Today, there were only nine, minus herself, plus *that* guy.

Granted, April wasn't May, and April wasn't June, and she should expect the number of customers to increase through the summer to make up for any shortage of customers now.

Still, she could do without that one customer.

Then again, he had paid for the tour.

There he was now, a smirk on his face as he sat down on a bench closer to the front, just one row behind the handicapped seats.

Through the window, Tamsyn could see that he was on his phone, as if this was just part of his agenda today, something to be checked off—

Oh, I don't know. I'm just making that up!

Tamsyn sighed. What was happening to her? Usually she was less judgmental. Today she was up in arms against a man she barely knew except in videoconferences.

But he wanted to demolish her beloved city block!

She sniffed, drew a deep breath, and put on her

signature tricorn hat.

She stepped onto the trolley and turned on her portable waistband microphone headset, telling herself to ignore the man only feet away from her, now looking at her intently.

"Welcome to Savannah, y'all!" she spoke into her headset. "I'm so glad you're here on this beautiful April day. Let's make some introductions, and then I'll tell you what we're going to do."

Tamsyn asked everyone to say where they were from. She wasn't surprised to hear that people had come from near and far. Some were Georgians, Floridians, Americans. But some others were from England, Germany, Korea, Australia, South Africa —and there was a family from the Maldives.

She made a note of all that information on her iPad. Later, when she had a minute, she'd pin a little flag from the Maldives to her world map on the wall of the Tamsyn Tours office.

Someday she would like to visit all those places. *Someday.*

"All right, ladies and gentlemen," Tamsyn continued. "As you know, this is a semi-walking tour through six colonial-era squares. I say *semi* because we're going to be dropped off and picked up at a couple of spots. This is for those who don't want to walk all the way."

There was much cheering and rejoicing in the

trolley.

"We're going to start with Ellis Square, then Johnson, Reynolds, Oglethorpe, Wright, and Telfair, which was originally named James Square. How many of you have been to all these squares?"

There were just a couple of people who had been to Savannah before and gone everywhere. Tamsyn nodded to the driver, who started easing the Tamsyn Tours trolley into the midmorning Savannah traffic.

Tamsyn stepped forward, suddenly aware that she was standing right next to Ryan. The bench seat in front of him was empty. She tried to pretend like he wasn't there.

But she couldn't miss the way he was staring at her.

His wavy hair was dark brown, and he had on another killer plaid shirt.

Tamsyn had always had a thing for men in plaid—

She cleared her throat. "One of the squares we're stopping at is Oglethorpe Square. Can anyone here tell me who General James Edward Oglethorpe was?"

Someone raised his hand. "The founder of Georgia."

"Excellent. He was one of the Trustees of Georgia." Tamsyn eased into her favorite historical period. "General James Oglethorpe was born in England in 1696, rose to prominence there, and was involved in politics. Does anyone here know what a debtors' prison is?"

No one did.

Seriously?

"Well, way back when in England, if you couldn't pay your debts, you'd be thrown into prison until your debts were paid off."

Ryan laughed. "How on earth were they going to do that if they were in prison?"

"Exactly. A seventeenth-century catch-22, if you will. Often they would borrow money from rich relatives or languish in prison. Well, a friend of General Oglethorpe ended up in that sad situation, and Oglethorpe was aware of such a thing."

Tamsyn stepped back. "Oglethorpe, Sir John Percival, and a bunch of other people in the British Parliament decided to do something about the injustice. And so we have the Georgia Charter."

"Bring me your tired and poverty-stricken huddled masses?" Ryan asked.

Oh boy. Tamsyn wondered how to answer that.

Should she have said something else?

You misquoted Emma Lazarus?

Wrong era, dude?

She decided to ignore him.

"Interestingly, the people who came in that first

ship to Georgia weren't from debtors' prisons." Tamsyn checked her location. The trolley was coming to a stop. She had to wrap it up.

"They were city folks, ordinary people, what England back then would call the working class," she said. "You see, Georgia was not only a place of opportunity for those first colonists, but it was a barrier land between Charles Towne—the old name for Charleston—and the Spanish forces south of it in Florida."

There were some remarks from the tourists.

"Most people in the debtor's prisons were sickly. They weren't physically able to work." Tamsyn continued. "You see, they needed settlers who could work the land, grow silk, and send fabric back to England to help the economy of their motherland. And to take up arms in case of Spanish attacks, which we'll talk more about if you take day-trip excursion tours to Fort Frederica on St. Simon's Island."

"So the first Georgian settlers were human shields," Ryan stated rather loudly. "Did most of them die?"

Tamsyn was caught off-guard by his remark as the trolley screeched to a halt by Oglethorpe Square.

She stared at him, dumbfounded.

Oh dear. This is going to be a long walking tour.

CHAPTER FIVE

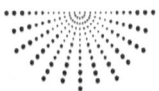

"*T*wenty percent off with any Tamsyn Tour tickets, you said." Ryan Ruttledge followed Tamsyn up the ramp to the *Caleigh Pendegrast* riverboat that Friday night. He liked walking alongside her. She had long strides, but he matched hers perfectly. "I went on the walking tour this morning, remember?"

Tamsyn frowned.

"You don't seem too happy to get another customer for the dinner cruise."

"Tonight's special cruise is for couples," Tamsyn explained. "One Friday a month, Dad reserves the entire riverboat for couples only."

That stopped Ryan in his tracks. "Hiroki!"

"Who?"

"Only my best bud—or perhaps, ex-best bud."

Ryan grunted. "He signed me up for this dinner cruise. He said he called your office this afternoon and booked a seat for me."

Tamsyn smiled.

Somehow Ryan didn't like that particular smile.

"Two seats, you mean," she said. "This is a couples' cruise, like I said. I'm sorry. And even with the twenty percent discount—for one ticket, let's say —you still paid more than everyone else if you didn't bring a date."

"Well, I don't care about the cost. I care that my friend did this to me." Ryan wondered what to do. He felt out of place with his three-piece suit. He looked ridiculous, like a clown. "Of all the Friday evening cruises in the year, I'm here tonight."

"Without a date. Poor thing."

Then it dawned on him. "You're by yourself too."

"I'm the tour guide. I don't count."

"We can sit together. I won't take up space." Ryan opened the door for her.

"You're in my space," Tamsyn said. Her eyes widened. "Sorry."

"You keep putting your foot in your mouth."

"No, I don't."

"But with me, you do."

"Why, you—"

A tourist stopped her. "Could you take our picture, please?"

"Sure." Tamsyn seemed too eager to get away from Ryan.

Trying not to feel hurt, Ryan looked around, as if searching for something.

Maybe I am searching for something...

Someone.

The maître d'hôtel greeted him. "May I seat you, sir?"

"Yes."

"And you're with?"

"Tamsyn Pendegrast."

"Oh." His eyes lit up.

Ryan found that amusing. But what did it mean? Did the maître d'hôtel's eyes look excited because he thought that Tamsyn had a date tonight? Was that uncommon for her? Or was that too common?

"This way, sir." Smiling, the maître d' ushered Ryan to a table in the back of the dining room. "Miss Pendegrast usually sits here. Alone."

His emphasis on *alone* answered all of Ryan's questions. "Well, she won't be alone this evening."

"I'm happy for her. About time." The maître d' waltzed away.

Whatever does that mean?

Ryan sat down and waited. He wondered if

Tamsyn would sit somewhere else if she saw him here. He looked around and spotted her chatting animatedly with some people.

He decided to leave the dining room until it was time to eat, and then he would return to his seat to—hopefully!—find Tamsyn there next to him.

On the open deck, the night air was cool, just the way he liked it. It wasn't chilly or balmy. It was in between winter and summer, as if warm air was about to burst out of its southern bubble, but not quite.

He checked his iPhone for the weather report, happily noting that it was in the lower sixties.

I like this place.

His dark blazer blocked the occasional wind sweeping up and down the Savannah River. He could hear the waves lapping against the riverboat hull. He placed both elbows on the railing and breathed in the night air.

"Nice out here," Ryan said to no one.

"I agree."

Ryan smiled. Loved that voice.

Euphonious...

He tipped his head to one side. "Nice of you to join me."

"I came to tell you that the evening's program is about to start, and since you paid for two, I don't want you to miss it." Tamsyn hesitated. "And..."

"And?" Ryan leaned against the railings. Waited.

"And I need to apologize for being snappy with you when we came up the ramp."

"Bad day, huh?"

"Long day, but there's no excuse, really. You're a customer of Tamsyn Tours, and I shouldn't be wearing my emotions on my sleeves."

"Your frustrations, you mean."

"No need to rub it in."

"Let's put business aside and enjoy our dinner, shall we?" Ryan motioned for Tamsyn to lead the way.

As she stepped ahead of him, Ryan placed his hand on the small of her back. She didn't have an ounce of fat underneath that evening sheath, modestly long enough to cover her knees. She wasn't bony either. She was—

Just right.

Ryan felt shallow that he had noticed her physical features. But he was confident there was more to her, way more, and he was intrigued.

CHAPTER SIX

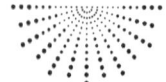

*I*t was one of those after-dinner giveaways that Dad loved to offer couples who had been married the longest, traveled the farthest, had the most kids or grandkids, and so forth. The prizes inevitably included another cruise on the *Caleigh Pendegrast* riverboat in the future, getting people to return to Savannah to collect their treats.

Dad loved to talk about Mom, and it broke Tamsyn's heart every time he did it. He'd tell the people at dinner about how he had met Caleigh Robinson way back in high school, how they had been high school sweethearts, how they had been married for thirty-some years before cancer had taken his dear Caleigh, now in heaven, waiting for him to go walk the streets of gold with her.

Tamsyn felt sorry for her dad. He was only sixty-three years old, too young to be a widower.

Then again, he'd probably say he felt sorry for her too. She had been barely nineteen when Mom passed away.

Eight years now and counting...

Tamsyn didn't realize her eyes were misty, until a warm hand squeezed her cold fingers under the table.

She was startled.

It was Ryan's hand.

She looked at him. His eyes were on hers, those darkish eyes that looked like he was perpetually smiling. His lips seemed like they were opening to say something but didn't.

He just held her hand.

Somehow that was enough for her.

Tamsyn sniffled.

The applause jolted her out of their moment of understanding. She pulled her hand away from Ryan's.

"I'm sorry," Ryan said.

What did he mean?

Was he sorry he had held her hand?

Was he sorry her mom had passed away? Was he sorry for her? Was he sorry he was taking away her childhood home?

Was he sorry she was fighting a lost cause? Was

he sorry that the city of Savannah was about to agree that the entire city block she lived on was not sustainable—livable!—without major renovations?

Tamsyn felt hot, like she needed to go outside to get some air.

Yet she couldn't leave. Dad would see her go, and he'd think—again!—that he had offended his only daughter, his little girl.

Always his little girl.

So Tamsyn sat there in silence, waiting for Dad's droning to stop and for him to call it a night.

"Caleigh and I thought we were going to have a passel of kids. Alas, the good Lord only gave us one biological child, and even though it took us fifteen years and several miscarriages, what a delight that child has been to me."

Child?

Dad!

Tamsyn tried to keep her cool. Something else Dad said affected her.

The good Lord.

Dad called God the good Lord.

Tamsyn's heart melted. Dad had come such a long, long way. It had taken many years of prayer before Dad had accepted Jesus as his personal Lord and Savior.

"You've all met my lovely daughter, Tamsyn, after whom I named this tour company, and who now runs it." Dad lifted his hand and pointed in her direction.

Tamsyn smiled as she always did, the dutiful daughter of a father in mourning for eight years now since Mom had passed. She had to be strong for him, to show him that life could go on even with Mom in heaven.

That was the thing.

For the first seven years since Mom had passed, Dad could not believe that Mom had gone to heaven to be with Jesus. He had called Christianity a fable and God a figment of man's imagination. Dad had believed that God was a man-made crutch.

Tamsyn had exhausted all the ways of telling Dad about God, how God loved him so much that He had sent His only Son, Jesus Christ, to save him from his sins.

It had been difficult for Dad to comprehend because he didn't believe he had sinned at all.

In fact, Dad believed he had lived a terrifically great life. What more could one ask for than to be able to live on a cruise ship the rest of his days!

Then Tamsyn had started attending Riverside Chapel, back when the church met at a storefront down River Street. Pastor Diego Flores had visited Dad on his riverboat, witnessed to him, and just like that, after over twenty years of people praying for him, Dad got saved.

His entire eternal future had changed with that moment in time.

So had his perspective. For one, he stopped working on Sundays, and he donated his other riverboat to be used for Riverside Chapel Sunday services.

Since then, the church had thrived with its very visible location.

"Come up here, Tam." Dad's voice filled the dining room.

What?

Tamsyn hadn't been paying attention.

Ryan leaned toward her and whispered in her ear. "He has a surprise for you."

"Oh. Thanks." *I owe you one.*

The last thing she wanted was to owe Ryan Ruttledge V anything.

Tamsyn placed her dinner napkin on the table as Ryan stood up to help her get out of her seat.

What a gentleman.

The thought was not lost on her as she made her way toward her beaming dad, who held a prettily wrapped pink box—of something—in his hands some five or six tables away.

CHAPTER SEVEN

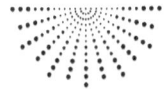

amsyn was weeding and watering her side garden early Saturday morning when a thought hit her. The opportunity had been there all day Friday, but she hadn't seen it until now.

That's it.

Ryan Ruttledge had signed up for a slew of tours. He had told her he wanted to get to know Savannah.

She had taken it in a hostile manner—perhaps in the most un-Christian way—and had accused him of the most nefarious reasons to be in town.

She had been convinced he was bent on her destruction.

Maybe if she had given him more history lessons, he wouldn't tear down the city block she was trying to preserve. Maybe if she had appealed to his sense of family, it could sway him to her point of view that history had to be preserved for posterity.

Never forget where you come from.

Never forget your history.

And history was all around her with the old Queen Anne style house that had been handed down through several Pendegrast generations since its construction in the late nineteenth century. Tamsyn had found wallpaper dating back to 1898 and forgotten quilts from the mid-1800s in the attic.

Next door, when the neighbor had been digging in his yard, he had uncovered traces of homes from the eighteenth century before the first Savannah fire in 1796 that had burned the city to the ground. After the second Savannah fire in 1820, this city block had been parceled out and sold to various people, including the Pendegrast family.

There was more history there that perhaps no one would be interested in unless his or her last name was Pendegrast.

Tamsyn sighed. Her middle name was her great-grandmother's first name.

Tamsyn Rosa Pendegrast.

"Yep. I'm the keeper—the only keeper—of the family history and heirlooms."

Among her prized possessions was an old type-writer that one of Rosa Pendegrast's aunts had used, now in a Savannah bank vault for safekeeping since the rash of burglaries and vandalism in this area. A QWERTY typewriter, no less, it was an 1892 North's model shipped from London. A number of Pendegrast ladies had been quite literary.

Yes, I should finish writing that book about my family history before this place is gone.

Gone.

She couldn't imagine it, but it could happen if RYUCP had its way. They were known for their sleek, modern, award-winning—huh!—commercial buildings that destroyed skylines. Glass cages and cold steel structures with no heart, no warmth—

Her iPhone rang. Tamsyn reached for it with her gloved hands and dropped the iPhone into the flower bed, soaked through with water.

Yikes.

She wiped it on her shorts, and now her shorts were covered with dirt and grime.

The phone stopped ringing.

She checked the voice mail.

"Oh no." She listened to the rest of the message from Mike. Unbelievable. Her Saturday tour guide was sick with the stomach flu. "I sure hope he didn't get it from the dinner cruise last night."

Her phone said she had twenty minutes before Mike's tour began.

She tapped to her schedule. Beatrice had started her tour, no doubt. Joe was conducting the ten o'clock Architectural Tour. Sandra was off for the day.

That left Tamsyn to fill in. No way was Dad doing this. His bad knees wouldn't last fifty yards on the Historic Homes Walking Tour.

"Mike! Why did you wait until the last minute to tell me you can't make it?" Tamsyn ran up the back stairs to get to her bedroom to shower and get dressed.

She wasn't sure how she was going to make it in twenty minutes.

Mike was covering for the front office too. Joe could be there early. He wasn't usually, but she could call him.

She rang his number.

No answer.

"Lord Jesus, don't let me get into a wreck on the way there!"

CHAPTER EIGHT

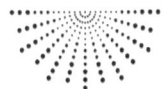

"*T*amsyn Tours. How may I help you?" Ryan said into the phone in between bites of donuts. He swiped his iPad, and found the Tamsyn Tours website and its listing of weekday local tours. "Monday, ma'am? Yes, there are several Historic Home Tours on Mondays."

From the corner of his eyes, he heard the door fling open, bells jangling, and Tamsyn Pendegrast appeared in the foyer.

Her damp hair was plastered to her head on one side and disheveled on the other side—as if she had toweled it off while driving here—and her face looked like a bewildered wild-eyed cat that had come out of a bathtub.

She was wearing a pretty blouse and a pair of

denim Bermuda shorts that exposed her legs all the way to her hiking boots.

In that second, Ryan forgot he was on the phone.

"Huh? Yeah—yes." He snapped to attention. "There's a tour at ten o'clock. Would you like me to pencil you in for that?"

He nodded into the phone as he jotted another name and number on a Post-it note. He was sticking the seventh or eighth sticky note on the glass table in chronological order when he looked up into the prettiest eyes in the southern USA.

"What are you doing?" Tamsyn asked. Those once-pretty eyes now shot daggers of "Get off my desk!" at him.

"Answering your phone. You're welcome." He lifted a donut out of the box at the edge of the table. "Want one?"

"Where's Joe?"

"Joe who? I don't know the people who work for you, okay? When I got here, some woman with a streak of green hair on one side and orange on the other drove away a trolley of customers, and nobody else was here. The phone started ringing, and here I am."

"I owe you another one."

"That's right. You owe me big time. And this time it's dinner."

"We had dinner last night. How about free tours?"

"I've already paid for my tour packages through next week."

"Isn't it a bit much to be taking all the tours we offer?" Tamsyn asked.

Ryan studied her to see how he should take that question, how he should answer it. He decided to err on the side of history. "Immersion. If I know more about Savannah, then I'll know how to..."

How to what?

He wasn't sure, exactly. How to tear down that city block that Tamsyn held so dear? How to renovate it to make it fit for the future?

Listen to me. How do I know what the future looks like?

Tamsyn's face reddened.

Ryan saw pain. The last thing he wanted to do was cause her pain.

He opened his mouth to speak, but she didn't give him a chance. She walked away from the front desk toward the group of tourists waiting in the sitting area.

Ryan followed her.

"Ladies and gentlemen, sorry for the delay. Your tour guide, Mike, is sick, so let's hope he gets well soon. I'm filling in for him on this tour, and we're going to get started as soon as we do a head count. Did anyone here just walk in?"

She nodded to the two or three people lifting up their hands.

"This Historic Homes Walking Tour is forty-five dollars per person, and we take cash, credit card, or PayPal. If you will just see me, we'll get your names on the tour list, and off we'll go. Thank you again for waiting."

Ryan stepped closer to Tamsyn. He had read the advertisement. It had said they would get maps. They were part of the deal.

Yeah, he had an eye for details, and it looked like Tamsyn needed some assistance. "Maps?"

"Maps?" Tamsyn pointed to the counter. "Ladies and gentlemen, Ryan here will hand out some maps in case anyone needs one, and in case your cell phone runs out of battery and you can't access your GPS."

Ryan felt rather helpful today. He tried to think of how else he could help Tamsyn in her predicament. The front desk was still unoccupied. If he offered to stay behind, he would miss the tour. Not only had he paid for the tour, he'd rather be with Tamsyn.

He caught himself.

It's true. I'd rather be with Tamsyn here in Savannah than anywhere else.

At this time? Or at any time?

More for him to pray about.

He wondered when these feelings had begun. It couldn't have been months before when RYUCP had offered the city of Savannah a deal to revitalize that street corner. It couldn't have been when the city officials had made the decision not to exercise their eminent domain privileges, but to let the homeowners be persuaded to sell instead.

Truly, that entire city block should have been condemned.

RYUCP could turn that place around and make it great again.

And yet...

Now he wondered if his fight for the future was worth breaking Tamsyn's heart for the past.

Three days before, there had been no question it was worth it.

Now?

He wasn't sure anymore.

CHAPTER NINE

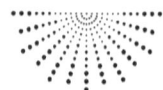

"*W*hat's wrong with a bit of old and a bit of new?" Tamsyn muttered as she picked up her Bible and notebook from the dining table where she had sat during the Sunday morning church service at Riverside Chapel.

She felt a warm breath on her neck and a whisper in her ear. "You mumble."

Tamsyn didn't say a word as she found Ryan inches away from her face, amusement in his eyes.

"Lunch on me?" he asked.

"Are you asking me out?"

"No. Everybody's going to lunch at Piper's Place. I only offered to pay for yours."

"Because?"

"Because I want to."

"To bribe me?" Tamsyn stuffed her Bible and

notebook into the canvas Tamsyn Tours tote bag.

"Bribe? For what?"

"For my childhood home you want to raze to the ground." Her voice cracked. Yes, that was exactly what Ryan and his company wanted to do to her family, to her, to her posterity.

Ryan raised an eyebrow. "Is that all you think about? On a Sunday, no less? The Lord's Day?"

"It's a big deal to me. A very big deal."

"Something you'd lose your appetite over?"

"More than that, I'd be devastated if I lose my family home."

"Devastated?"

"It's the truth." Tamsyn moved away from Ryan, who stood there rooted to the floor, looking hurt and somewhat dejected. She resisted feeling sorry for him.

"*D*evastated. She said devastated." Ryan made a face into the FaceTime camera on his iPhone as he relaxed on his fourth-floor hotel room balcony facing the afternoon wind coming over Savannah. Below the cantilevered deck floor, the streets were busy with people and vehicles.

"That bothered you because..." Hiroki laughed, his face filling Ryan's iPhone.

Hiroki seemed to be laughing a lot lately, and had continued laughing even as Ryan gave him an earful about setting him up for the dinner cruise without a date.

If his friend from architectural school kept on that route, Ryan wouldn't be sure who was directing his path and decisions. Was it God working through Hiroki? Or was Ryan himself winging it?

"I don't want to cause her pain," Ryan said.

"We sent you to Savannah for a bit of an R & R and a scouting expedition, man. We didn't send you there to buddy up with your nemesis."

"She's not my nemesis."

"She was that and more on Thursday morning. What happened between then and now?"

Love happened.

There. He had thought it.

"So what are you going to do, Ryan Ruttledge? Got a plan?"

Ryan bristled. "Why don't you give me a plan? You got me into this mess."

"Me? You agreed to it."

Yeah, I did. "But still, if you hadn't—"

"Wait a minute, Ryan." Hiroki leaned back.

It was then that Ryan saw where Hiroki was: at his desk. "Did you go to church this morning?"

"Sure did. I brought a change of clothes and got takeout for lunch. Why?"

"Just want to make sure you didn't pull another all-nighter." Ryan was relieved. He didn't want anyone in the office working on Sundays. He firmly believed that if his business partners and employees had a day of rest, they'd be more productive during weekdays.

"No. I just had some extra work to do. I promise to be done in a few hours."

"Maybe I should get home tonight," Ryan said. "We have that Urquhart project in Alpharetta we need to tweak."

"And one in Chattanooga too."

"Right."

"No, don't talk yourself into it. You have another week. Take advantage of it and get some rest. You work harder than the rest of us, Ryan, and you deserve time off."

"It doesn't feel like time off. It feels like I'm goofing off."

"Well, things are moving around here even without you."

Ryan shook his head. "Some job security I have, then."

"Ha-ha. Look, we'll see you in a week," Hiroki said. "Rest up. Big days ahead."

Big days ahead, indeed.

Soon, Ryan would have to disclose his feelings for Tamsyn while pulling the house from her. He

knew nothing good could come out of their relationship. It was a dead end because they could not agree
on Rosa Pendegrast Lane.

Ryan said goodbye to Hiroki. He decided to go
for a run. Around the blocks a few times should
clear his head and give him some perspective.

No.

His perspective had to come from God alone.

Quietly, Ryan prayed.

*Lord Jesus, I need Your wisdom in this matter
about Tamsyn. Guard us in this situation, whether
the outcome is good or bad for both of us.*

No sooner had he prayed than Ryan remembered that God had His best in mind for both him
and Tamsyn.

Both? I'm including her now?

Ryan looked up the verse he knew well. Jere-
miah 29:11 popped up rather quickly on his Bible
app. He asked Siri to read it.

> *For I know the thoughts that I think toward you,
> says the Lord, thoughts of peace and not of evil, to
> give you a future and a hope.*

Ryan nodded, agreeing with the Bible.

Thoughts of peace. That's what I want.

*Peace with Tamsyn and, more importantly, peace
with God.*

CHAPTER TEN

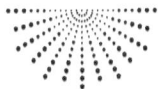

"You baffle me, Tamsyn." Ryan Ruttledge had been sticking to her side ever since they boarded the HMS *Charity* for the hour-long tour. The rest of the tour group was scattered throughout the tall ship.

"How so?" Tamsyn walked past the mizzenmast toward the quarterdeck, her footfall quiet against the wooden deck.

"You love those old colonial days, and yet you said the other day that you fear the ocean."

"I never said that to you," Tamsyn protested.

"Not to me, but to another tourist on a trolley tour."

Tamsyn wondered how to respond to that. "Just because you take all my tours doesn't mean you should listen in on my conversations with others."

"Well, I was right there."

"Eavesdropping is a bad idea. You might mishear something."

"I didn't mishear your fear of the ocean, did I?" Ryan asked.

Tamsyn bristled.

Ryan waved his arms about. "This tall ship sails the oceans."

"It's docked," Tamsyn said, wondering what Ryan was driving at.

"Right now. And this is as far as you go."

"What about my riverboat tours?"

"Those are not on open seas," Ryan pointed. "You're on a river—this river—flanked by land."

"What are you saying?" Tamsyn tilted her head so she could stare into his eyes.

Want a fight?

"You won't venture out of your comfort zone." Ryan's smile was both teasing and taunting.

Tamsyn wasn't sure how to defend herself.

"I'm happy on land," she managed.

Ryan stepped toward her, close enough to make Tamsyn a tad nervous. It didn't help that his lips beckoned her to go where she wasn't sure she should.

"I'm asking you to set your sails," he said.

"Whatever for?" Tamsyn stepped back. It was a feeble attempt at retreating, and she knew it.

"See the possibilities."

"Possibilities, Ryan? They could be as ugly as your ghastly buildings—"

Oops.

Her palm flew to her mouth. "I didn't mean to say..."

There was nowhere for Tamsyn to hide. They were on an open deck. All around Ryan and her, tourists walked to and fro, chattering in many languages. Their voices wove into a polyphony that rose into the spring morning and dissipated into the Atlantic winds above the tall ship.

"I stepped out of the norms. I created something different, new." Ryan wasn't done speaking. "You never left the bluff, so to speak. Me? I unfurled my sails. I went out there."

Tamsyn snapped back to her usual self. "Yeah, and you ventured where no common sense has gone before."

"Common sense?" Ryan asked. "Let me show you what common sense is."

Ryan lifted her hand and kissed it gently.

His lips were soft.

Oh, so soft.

"That's common sense." Ryan stepped into Tamsyn's shadow in the morning light, his eyes still fixed on hers.

"You make no sense," Tamsyn said.

"Nonsense, you say?" Gently, Ryan's thumb rubbed her chin.

His thumb is soft too!

Does this guy ever do dishes?

Tamsyn was surprised at what had just popped into her head. Dishes? What on earth would make her think of something domestic at a moment like this?

Before she could parse her way back to what was happening, Ryan's warm lips were on hers, tasting like Burt's Bees coconut lip balm.

She surprised herself by enjoying his affection.

It ended too soon.

"That, I don't normally do." Ryan stepped back. "Hence, to me, that was uncommon sense."

CHAPTER ELEVEN

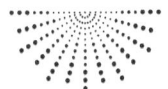

*R*yan watched Tamsyn's stunned hazel eyes soften into what looked like part bewilderment and part surprise.

He turned and walked away, his shoulder muscles feeling warm, as though she was staring at his back more intensely than the midmorning sun.

His palms turned clammy and he could hear his own heartbeats.

Yep. Definitely uncommon sense.

Something was happening between Tamsyn and him, but he wasn't sorry he had rocked her boat.

He sought her out the rest of the tour, but she avoided him. Even when their tour group jostled for space in the galley, Tamsyn made sure she stood far enough away from him to avoid eye contact.

What? Was it my lip balm?

No more words were exchanged between them that morning, not even when they filed onto the trolley for the ride back to Tamsyn Tours.

Somehow, Ryan felt a longing he had never felt with any of his ex-girlfriends. Well, he hadn't had too many to begin with.

But Tamsyn Pendegrast was different.

He could still feel her lips on his own—her nervous but responsive lips.

Yes, she had responded to his kiss.

That was all he needed to know.

But is it all?

Had he prayed about this? Or was it an emotional reaction to Tamsyn's proximity? Leading her on would be damaging to both of them, especially in the eyes of God, wouldn't it?

He barely knew her. He didn't even know what brand of Christianity she believed. Well, it could go both ways. She didn't know what he believed. Perhaps that was why Tamsyn had stayed away from him after their encounter by the mizzenmast.

And then there was the matter of Rosa Pendegrast Lane that stood between them, a gulf that might be too wide to cross.

The unmistakable ringtone that came from Ryan's shorts pocket startled him. He would have welcomed it if not for what had transpired between him and Tamsyn. Now he dreaded what Jared was going to say to him.

Even though putting off the inevitable could make it worse, Ryan decided to ignore the call from Jared Urquhart, another business partner and the one holding the RYUCP purse strings.

He heard the little ping. Jared's call had gone to voice mail.

Good.

Then he heard another tone.

A text message.

All right, all right.

Ryan reached into his pocket to retrieve the iPhone. He promptly regretted reading it.

We got the other two houses. You made any progress with that Pendegrast woman?

Something about that text message rubbed Ryan the wrong way.

It wasn't that Jared had called Tamsyn "that Pendegrast woman."

It wasn't that RYUCP had somehow managed to wrangle the other two houses out of their home-owners' hands. He was sure Jared had offered them deals they could not resist, perhaps beach houses and such things that Jared's influences could procure.

But what made Ryan feel disgusted and dirty was what Jared had implied he was doing in Savannah. He wasn't here to "make any progress" with Tamsyn—at least not in the way he had expected.

All he came here to do was to understand why Tamsyn Pendegrast held on to her childhood home like a tenacious pit bull. She knew it was an old house. She knew it would take a lot of money to renovate and restore it, something along the order of a few hundred thousand dollars or more, depending on the condition of the house. From the photographs Ryan had seen, Tamsyn's house was in rather shabby condition.

And yet, she would not let it go.

What about the memories of the place that had so permeated her?

Beyond that, Ryan didn't really have a proper agenda. Hiroki had one—study the opposition. But now that Ryan had spent some time with Tamsyn, he no longer viewed her as his opposition. On the contrary, he wanted to spend more time with her.

Not for business reasons, but for something more personal.

Ryan chided himself. He should have sorted out his feelings before he kissed Tamsyn earlier in the tour. Now there was a barrier between them.

Still, he had kissed her because he wanted to. Did she know that?

CHAPTER TWELVE

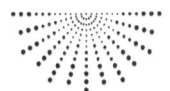

"*I*'ve been blindsided. I can't believe my neighbors caved in." Tamsyn buried her face in her hands as she sank into the rattan couch in Heidi's sunroom. "They want money more than history."

"Tam, let's not judge," Heidi Wei-Flores said as she turned on the fan. "We need to trust God to handle this."

Above Tamsyn, the fan whirled away the warm breeze. Through the open windows facing the backyard, she could hear the ocean beyond the dunes. The afternoon waves were so loud it felt like they were crashing up against her rib cage.

Can't breathe!

Heidi sat down next to her and rubbed her

shoulders. "I would tell you it's all going to be okay, but until then, it's a rough road we'll need to travel."

Tamsyn nearly chuckled. "Trust you to tell me as it is, but this is not your road. This is mine."

"You're my friend and sister in Christ. I'm your prayer support. I'm not the only one. Nadine, Sabine, Abilene—"

"Say, did you know all their names rhyme?"

"Focus, Tam."

"Right." And then and there, Tamsyn lost it. "I thought if we formed Save Old Savannah and petitioned RYUCP to leave us alone, they would go away."

"They can't make you sell your house."

"But look at the pressure. Everyone in the city block has given in. I'm next."

"You can hold out."

"For how long?" After Tamsyn ran out of tears, she reached for the glass of water that seemed to appear in front of her. "Thank you. You're very thoughtful, Heidi."

"No worries," Heidi said. "Now tell me. Is Ryan Ruttledge the one pressuring you to sell? I can ask Ming to get you some legal counsel."

"Ryan? No, he's not pressuring me. Oh, I don't know. He hasn't left town. Do you think—maybe? Maybe he's here to pressure me." Tamsyn paused. He had been charming. Sly!

"Wait. I didn't mean to suggest it. I'm simply asking, verifying. You know we historians ask a lot of questions."

"Maybe I haven't asked enough." Tamsyn's brows furrowed. "From Friday through yesterday, he went on a number of tours with us. I couldn't turn him away. He was a paying customer."

"And you don't have enough tour guides to let someone else deal with him."

"Right." Tamsyn finished drinking her water. She sat back on the couch, folding her arms tightly around her chest. She wanted to sink into a cave and hide in the dark.

But she knew she had to face this head on.

Heidi didn't smile. "The way I look at it, both of you have conflicts of interest."

"Both of us?"

Heidi nodded. "His company wants to buy your house, your city block. You don't want to sell. You two are at opposite ends. How does the tension feel when both of you are on the same trolley?"

Ironically, Tamsyn enjoyed seeing Ryan. The way Ryan behaved, she thought he might have enjoyed seeing her too.

Or maybe he was looking for a way to push my buttons.

Tamsyn sighed. "I don't have to sell my private property if I don't want to."

"Right. But the pressure is there," Heidi said. "Now RYUCP has bought every single house on that block except yours while Ryan Ruttledge is touring old-town Savannah."

"I thought maybe I could convert him, make him see that history is not all that bad. Family history, hometown history, they're all worth preserving. I wanted to share how easy it is to balance the past and present. It needn't be one or the other."

"And?"

"I thought he might come around." Tamsyn's lips tingled as she remembered their moment on the tall ship.

What happened there?

Was it genuine?

"Something happened? Something unexpected?"

"Yes." Tamsyn admitted it more to herself than to Heidi.

"You two started developing some sort of rapport."

"More than that." Tamsyn didn't meet Heidi's eyes. "We sort of clicked."

"Clicked in what say?"

"In a heartfelt way, let's just say."

"Like you've moved beyond your videoconference calls."

"Something like that." Tamsyn didn't want to confess that she had let her guard down. Oh boy, had she let her guard down. "It felt real. He felt real."

"But you're not sure."

"He could be the wrong guy, Heidi."

"Is he?" Heidi smiled. "To you, Tam, they're all wrong guys. That's why you haven't dated in years."

"Only because I've been busy with Tamsyn Tours."

"Uh-huh."

"What does that mean?"

"Sometimes God brings unexpected warmth in the middle of wintry cold."

Tamsyn stared at her friend. "Is that why Pastor Flores married you?"

"What do you mean?"

"You say the most profound things." Tamsyn knew what Heidi had meant.

In spite of being a successful businesswoman, Tamsyn had been alone for a very long time. Perhaps this season, this beautiful springtime, her favorite time of the year, God had brought to her doorsteps a warm love for her.

"Diego talked to Ryan at church on Sunday," Heidi said.

"Yeah?"

"Twice, in fact. Once before the service, and once after." Heidi was thoughtful. "I think it was after you went home."

"Yeah, Ryan offered to pay for my lunch at Piper's. It wasn't necessary. It felt awkward. So I went to lunch elsewhere."

"If you want, I can ask Diego to call Ryan and speak with him."

"About what, Heidi?"

"To see what he's up to."

"Uh... No, I think I can handle this myself—with God's help." Tamsyn prayed to God that Ryan would turn out to be a good guy. "I sure hope there's no conspiracy to get me so distracted with his charm and charisma while his business partners buy up the rest of the city block, thus leaving me without support for my cause to save Rosa Pendegrast Lane."

"Who knows?" Heidi clasped Tamsyn's hands. "Let's pray and ask the Lord to show us what to do."

Tamsyn nodded. "You pray."

"Okay."

They both closed their eyes. Heidi took her time. She prayed Scripture back to God.

Outside the sunroom, the loud roar of waves seemed to calm down. Perhaps it was psychological, Tamsyn thought, but she was more apt to believe that God's peace was upon her.

"In Jesus Christ we have the peace of God," Heidi was saying. "No matter what happens to us—or to the properties and stuff we own—we know that our souls are eternally secure in heaven. Thank You, Lord, for the heavenly perspective for our earthly problems."

Yes, Lord, I need Your perspective.

After they prayed, Heidi pointed to a wall clock that showed it was almost time for them to eat their salad dinner and then go to Riverside Chapel for their Wednesday night church activities.

"Thank you for praying for me," Tamsyn said. She followed Heidi into the kitchen to help her get plates out of the cabinet.

"I'm glad it worked out," Heidi said. "Diego usually works at home Wednesdays so we can drive to the midweek service together, but this afternoon he has several counseling sessions. It's nice of you to give me a ride so that Diego and I don't need to drive separately tonight after church."

"What are friends for?"

Heidi closed the refrigerator. "Most of all, I do remind myself that no matter what people say, we need to do things God's way. God's wisdom is the key."

"You have a verse for me."

"God has a verse for you. Search the Bible and

ask God to show you an anchor verse that can help you through this time of uncertainty."

"I will." Tamsyn put down the plate. "In fact, I'll do it right now."

Very quickly, she searched her Bible app on her phone for the verse. She would much rather read a printed Bible, but when looking for verses, her Bible app made the search process go much faster. She would underline the verses in her study Bible, which she had left in her car parked outside.

At home, she preferred to read Mom's Bible, but that Bible never left the house. It was too fragile to be carted around to and from church.

"Here's one." She bookmarked it.

"Let's hear it." Heidi tossed the dark leafy green salad in a big bowl.

"It's from Proverbs 16:20."

> He who heeds the word wisely will find good,
> And whoever trusts in the Lord, happy is he.

"Good one. How about we both memorize it and see what God will do with it?"

"Sounds good to me." Tamsyn felt better already. Someone other than Dad sympathized with her problems.

God provides, doesn't He?

She loved her friends at Riverside Chapel. They genuinely cared for her.

Thank You, Lord, for loving me. You're all I need.

Take my house, if You so choose, Lord. I give it to You.

CHAPTER THIRTEEN

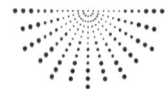

*R*yan Ruttledge found one parking spot several blocks away, put some coins into the slot, and doubled back to Rosa Pendegrast Lane.

He had seen the aerial view of this area and watched some videos of the changes from the end of its glory days in the seventies until today. He had read how various revitalization advocates had urged the city of Savannah to blot the decaying blight from its landscape.

Yet the homeowners prevailed.

Once, there had been more city residents—and even tourists and visitors—who had stood up with the homeowners, but in recent years, the number of supporters had dwindled to just the homeowners and local historians and preservationists.

Lately, the support had been reduced to the fledgling Save Old Savannah group more active on social media—as they chatted among themselves—than they were in real life, preserving old structures.

Surely that support would vanish now that only one unsold house remained on Rosa Pendegrast Lane: Tamsyn's house. As far as Ryan was concerned, the house wasn't worth saving if it couldn't even make it to the National Register of Historic Places.

So there, Tam. What do you say about that?

Ryan stopped in his tracks.

Did I just call her Tam?

Whoa. Getting too personal there?

Ryan brushed it off. He reached the street corner across from Tamsyn's house. He would have come sooner had he thought it wouldn't intrude into his friendship—or developing relationship—with Tamsyn.

But here he was.

He wanted to see for himself what would be lost.

"There's not much to see," Ryan said aloud. No one was around him.

The hundred-and-thirty-some-year-old Queen Anne was rundown. Its heyday was over. The old yellowish-and-brownish paint job on the ginger-bread-style trim covered the entire house. The roof looked new, but the wraparound porch—the veranda—was worn and weary. The house had some brick features, but it was mostly made of wood, particularly the veranda and the second floor.

He had expected more substantial brick in this house, but he hadn't been too familiar with the Victorian period. Another miss in history, he supposed.

The two houses that RYUCP had purchased were situated very close to the backyard of Tamsyn's house. In fact, only a magnolia tree and some trimmed azalea bushes separated the lots. The magnolia tree was as tall as Tamsyn's house, spread out, and took up most of her backyard.

Ryan crossed Rosa Pendegrast Lane.

There were very few people out and about this time of day. Ryan figured more people were at work. This side of town wasn't a tourist spot, after all.

He walked along the low hedges separating the sidewalk and the front of the house. The flower garden was pretty and had gobs of azaleas every-where, but compared to all other azalea gardens in Georgia, this garden was ordinary at best. Perhaps Tamsyn was too busy with her tour company to do anything beyond the basic maintenance. Perhaps her business didn't earn enough for her to fix up this house and spruce up the garden.

All in all, there was nothing remarkable about this property.

Ryan had seen better buildings than this. In fact, older private homes, lovingly restored, would have a better future than this rundown has-been.

And yet Tamsyn held on to it. Why?

She must really like the old-world charm.

Ryan, on the other hand, preferred modern and minimalist architecture with fewer bargeboards hanging off roofs. *Give me sleek, clean lines. Marble, steel, glass.*

Nothing ornate, please. And nothing this old.

He stood at the low gate leading up to the front door of the house. Tamsyn was probably at work, knowing her, and he was in no danger of being spotted.

As he slowly strolled the sidewalk, he surveyed the house again, looking for fault lines, for leanings. Surely the house was leaning somewhere. Against the blue sky, the chimney stood as stately as its creaky old self could.

"Look at all that efflorescence on the brick," Ryan mumbled. It was interesting that Tamsyn had left the whitish swaths on the old chimney. They reminded him of patina on copper steeples.

Such things didn't appeal to him at all.

Ryan counted four oak trees surrounding the

house. It would be a shame to cut them down. Perhaps they could keep the garden.

Yes, he'd talk to Jared and Hiroki about keeping the garden.

Get rid of that beat-up house. Keep the azaleas and the live oaks.

It would be the green thing to do.

Ryan stopped at the corner. Up on the second floor of the Victorian were a couple of *oeil-de-boeuf*, round windows that looked like portholes on a cruise ship.

There was nothing more to see beyond that. It was a small house on what could have been a prime city lot, had the neighborhood not been in such a poor condition.

That was where Ruttledge Yamada Urquhart Commercial Properties came in. They would fix up this entire area in no time. The mixed-use properties, new shops and condos, sports complexes, community fields, open green spaces, and whatever else investors could afford would certainly change history.

Meanwhile, this old house had to go.

"I'll bet it's grimy inside the house. Hundred-year-old grime." Ryan suspected there might even be asbestos and lead in there. Maybe even mold and fungus and other disease agents.

Give me sterile houses any day.

"No historical germs for me," Ryan concluded.

He was about to go back to his car when he saw the front door open. Out walked Tamsyn Pendegrast. She came to a screeching halt at the edge of her porch and stared straight at him.

"Go away," she said.

"Nice to see you too." Ryan stared.

Tamsyn looked feminine standing there in that colorful paisley summer dress. Ryan wanted to go to her, but he didn't move from the sidewalk.

"Why are you here?" she finally asked.

"I've never been here before."

"Why are you doing this to me?"

Oh boy, her voice is harsh.

Ryan tried to remain unaffected. "I like those oxeye windows in the back."

Tamsyn pursed her lips. She looked kinda cute—

"I'd better go," he said.

CHAPTER FOURTEEN

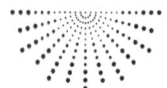

"*W*hy, Ryan?" Tamsyn asked to his back.

Ryan spun around.

"Why do you have to destroy the past?" Her voice was low, as if it had pained her to get the words out.

Ryan didn't like to hear such a sad voice. "Some things are worth preserving, and some are not."

"And my house, with all its history, is not worth preserving?"

"I'm not saying—"

"What are you saying, Ryan Ruttledge V?"

"I—uh..."

"Do you know what you're destroying?" Tamsyn snapped. "Memories. Memories of days gone by."

"Memories can be preserved regardless of where you are."

"This is a place of remembrance," Tamsyn said. "There are so many Pendegrast memories here, and in one stroke, you will destroy everything."

"Surely not everything."

"Everything I hold dear."

Oh.

"Then show me what you think you're losing." Ryan wasn't sure why he said it. The last thing he wanted to do was enter an old house. He hadn't brought any gloves, dust masks, or hand sanitizers.

"This entire house with everything in it," Tamsyn said.

"Okay."

"You want to see my house."

"I've already seen the outside." Still, Ryan wasn't exactly sure he wanted to go inside.

There are historical germs in there!

He had meant to only walk around this block to see for himself the one last property that would soon belong to RYUCP.

Soon? Yes. There was no way Tamsyn could hold on to this property.

Well, ironically, it would be entirely possible for this old house to be the only structure left from the nineteenth century on Rosa Pendegrast Lane.

It wouldn't be a total loss if that happened.

RYUCP still had the other ninety-six percent of the block.

"Yes?" Tamsyn asked.

"Huh?"

"Would you like to see this house before you raze it down?"

"We'll only do that if you sell the house to RYUCP. You can choose not to sell at all."

Tamsyn was visibly moved. "I'm tired of fighting, Ryan."

In fewer strides than he had expected, Ryan crossed the path and reached Tamsyn.

"Truth be told, I can't maintain this house. I'm only a small-business owner. I was praying—hoping against hope—that a historical society somewhere would restore this house and preserve it. I would give it up to them, but not to a commercial builder who wants to tear it down. There, I said it."

They looked at each other.

Then Ryan said, "I could use a cup of tea."

"Did you just invite yourself into my house twice?"

"Only if you can make proper tea. Not the tea bag kind, but loose leaf, preferably organic tea, steeped in boiling hot water in a teapot. If you can do that, then my mother will love you to death."

Tamsyn laughed. "Your mother?"

"She lives in Oxford."

"Mississippi?"

"England." Ryan chuckled.

"I didn't know your mom is English. Or maybe she's an expat?"

"She was born and grew up in the Cotswolds, but career-wise, she wrote for a travel magazine and toured the world."

"A writer."

"Retired."

"I would love to visit medieval towns in Europe. Someday." Tamsyn's eyes lit up, then fell. "Oh, I forget. You're not into old buildings and old places and ancient towns of yore. I don't mean to pry, but your distaste for history... Might that have come from your childhood?"

"How much does this session cost?" Ryan tried to make light of it. It had been decades since Mother had left him with Dad and had taken his younger sisters to England with her. Ryan had been little at that time—maybe four or five—and hadn't understood what went on.

To this day, Ryan and his sisters were not close. They hardly spoke to one another. Never emailed. They weren't friends on Facebook. For all practical purposes, it was like they had never been in the same family.

All Ryan could do was move forward. Onward to the future. There was no reason to look back—

Oh.

That explains it.

Ryan was too ashamed to look at Tamsyn. In one moment, she had exposed his heart and the reason it hadn't mattered to him one iota at all if old houses were destroyed to make way for new construction. He didn't want to remember the past.

Now his own personal gripe had spilled over to lovely Tamsyn.

Now he was about to destroy her memories just because his own were ripped away from him at an early age.

How could he possibly do that?

"Tea and tour?" Tamsyn asked again. She seemed to sense his loss, his emotions, and somehow, similar to what he had tried to do for her earlier, she now tried to lighten his load.

They seemed to complement each other.

"Sounds like a deal," Ryan said. "I'll take any hot tea you have."

"I have all kinds. Darjeeling, Earl Gray, Assam, Chai, Jasmine…" Tamsyn headed for the front door. "We can sit on the back porch and watch the grass grow."

Ryan laughed.

"Maybe we can figure out how to save this house." *Whoa.* Ryan caught himself. When had that thought formed in his heart?

Tamsyn stopped in her tracks. "Seriously?"

"If it means this much to you, I want you to be happy."

"Me? You're thinking of my happiness?"

"Yes, I want you to be happy."

"Sounds like this is going to be a pleasant afternoon." Tamsyn smiled. "God is good."

"He always is." Ryan glanced at his watch. "What about work? Don't you have to work?"

"You remember Mike, who called in sick with stomach flu last Saturday? He's filling in for me."

Ryan nodded. "The day I volunteered without pay at your office?"

"I'm paying you with a cup of hot tea."

"Fair enough." Ryan stopped at the front door and hesitated.

What about them thar historical germs?

Oh well.

He held the door for Tamsyn. "After you, ma'am."

CHAPTER FIFTEEN

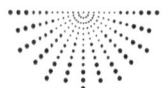

*T*he classic Queen Anne style house from the late nineteenth century was dark and old. That much, Tamsyn would admit. She led Ryan from the vestibule through the parlor and to the sitting room, where an ornate fireplace held court.

She watched him study the walls and ceilings and floors.

Ryan walked toward the fireplace and placed his hand on the ornate carvings leading to the mantel. An oval mirror hung on the wall on top of it.

In the mirror, Tamsyn saw Ryan's face. His eyes were on hers.

Self-conscious that her hair was undone, she looked away. "I spend a lot of time outdoors."

"I would too. It's very dark in here."

"Well, it's Victorian. What did you expect?"

"Don't you find that ironic?" Ryan walked toward an old settee, which pretty much an extra-long sofa to most people.

Tamsyn didn't think he'd be interested to know that the tapestry was Aubusson, brought from France some sixty or seventy years before the sofa was made.

"Ironic? In what way?" Tamsyn couldn't read his face anymore. It remained stoic.

"This house looks like a museum."

"It is a museum. I was hoping—dreaming—to restore it and make it part of our tour of homes and gardens."

"But?"

"It takes time and money to get there. I had some estimates, but even if I sold Tamsyn Tours, I couldn't afford the restoration. I do have some estimates, but I don't have the means."

"What about Save Old Savannah?"

"It's doing modest fund-raising to take out ads, but our sponsors emailed me saying Rosa Pendegrast Lane is a lost cause."

"I'm sorry."

"Well, you asked. Now you've heard my side of the story." Tamsyn pointed to the painting of a

happy couple above the settee. "Ebenezer Pendegrast commissioned that painting in 1820 for his
wife, who died several years later in childbirth,
together with their baby daughter."

She paused. "Ebenezer never remarried. After
he passed away without issue, his younger brother,
my great-great-grandfather, Henry Pendegrast,
brought the painting here when he built this house
in 1882."

"Lovely couple," Ryan said. "What did the
Pendegrast family do?"

"You mean their trade? They were sea
merchants, and that helped them survive after the
Civil War when railroads in Georgia had been deci-
mated. Farmers couldn't get any of their goods, like
cotton, to the port of Savannah. The Pendegrast
family continued to bring in goods from Europe and
Asia to sell to the locals."

When Ryan didn't reply, Tamsyn continued. "If
you must know, the Pendegrast family never traded
in slavery."

"Good to know."

"And my great-great-grandfather Henry married
a Cherokee."

"He did?"

Tamsyn nodded. "Unfortunately, Henry loved
to travel the world and sail the seven seas, so to
speak. He perished in the Indian Ocean in a storm,

leaving his widow to raise seven children on her own, one of them being Eugene Pendegrast, my great-grandfather, born in this house in 1890."

"You remember all that in your head?" Ryan asked.

"Dad said I should write it all down."

"Good idea. Then you can hand out brochures."

Tamsyn ignored him. "Twenty-nine years later, Eugene married Rosa Silverman in this very house, and five years after that, my grandfather, Wilbur Pendegrast, was born."

Ryan stood at the window. "The road out there is Rosa Pendegrast Lane."

"Yes. My great-grandmother was a philan-thropist before the stock market crashed in 1929. They had renamed the road after her because of her generosity to the city of Savannah and the surrounding coastal region. After the crash, well, everybody suffered."

Tamsyn took Ryan to the library on the other side of the sitting room. Every wall in the library was covered with bookshelves and books.

"Wow. Lots of books in here," Ryan said.

Tamsyn walked about. "These bookcases are original, made out of live oak wood from St. Simon's Island, the same type of oak they used to build the USS *Constitution*."

Ryan stepped forward to take a closer look at the spines of some of the books. Then he sneezed.

"Oh, please don't sneeze into those books. They're very old. Some are hundreds of years old. They belonged to my great-grandmother, who started the first collection."

"Sorry. I didn't mean to. It's just that it's—uh, a bit dusty in here."

"Let me show you something, and then we'll be out of here." Tamsyn went to a secretary. She opened a door below the desktop and produced an old Bible. "Check this out."

Ryan refused to touch it.

Tamsyn thought that was funny. "This Bible was printed in 1829. Nice, isn't it?"

"It looks old."

Tamsyn turned on the reading lamp sitting on the secretary and carefully opened the Bible for Ryan to see. He peeked.

"Live births and deaths," Ryan read aloud. "I wouldn't think you'd have live deaths."

"So you think there should be a comma there?" Tamsyn asked.

"I failed history, not English, in college."

Tamsyn let it pass.

"It should be in a museum, in some sort of temperature-controlled casing," Ryan said.

Tamsyn gave him a look. *Now he's talking.* "So you think it should be preserved."

Ryan nodded.

"For posterity."

"For our children's children."

"That's posterity, Ryan."

"I don't mean *our* children, literally, as in yours and mine—"

"I know what you meant: future generations."

"Right."

"So you don't hate history at all."

"Hate? That's a strong word," Ryan said.

"Then why tear down this city block?"

Ryan said nothing.

Tamsyn tried to continue the conversation, but she had nothing more to say to him either. Ryan would have to get it—understand it—himself.

Well, there was one thing she could say.

Somehow they had reached the renovated kitchen, and Tamsyn didn't remember how she had led Ryan there. She guessed it had been her usual route coming home from work. She'd dash straight into the kitchen to make herself dinner or a cup of tea. She could get there from the front door with her eyes closed, even zigzagging through the arches and narrow halls.

"I'll boil some water to make tea," Tamsyn announced.

"Is the tour over?" Ryan sounded disappointed.

"Pretty much. I don't think I'll show you the upstairs since my bedroom—chamber, as they called it way back when—is there, you know."

"I understand. No need. Are those stairs in the foyer the only way up?"

Tamsyn nodded.

"The narrow treads look treacherous."

"Tell me about it. I've slipped on them more times than I want to remember." In fact, Tamsyn had thought about those stairs more than any other elements of the old house. In cases of an emergency, this was the only flight of stairs down to safety from her bedroom.

That, or through the window upstairs—but first she had to take the emergency ladder out of the box it came in and read the instructions on how to lower it out the window.

She didn't want to think about climbing down a rope ladder.

Yikes.

She made a note to herself to figure out—as soon as possible—how to get out of her house through the second-floor window on her emergency ladder.

Today. After Ryan leaves.

"Tea?" she asked.

"Tea will be fine. Do you have crumpets?"

"Crumpets?" Why did he ask for crumpets?

Tamsyn decided to brush it off. It was pointless to try to understand a visitor to the city who would be going home soon.

"No, but I have shortbread cookies. Will that suffice?"

"Sure." Ryan looked around. "This kitchen is modern."

"Well, there was no way I was going to cook on an old stove circa World War II." Tamsyn folded her arms.

"You're a contradiction." Ryan laughed. "You talk about old things, but in this kitchen, you have brand-new appliances and they don't even look old-style."

"Something old, something new. I don't see why old and new cannot live together."

"That so?" Ryan stepped toward her. "If you come to Atlanta, look me up. I'll show you the future of architectural design."

Maybe it wasn't a bad idea to get a new perspective. "All right. That sounds fair."

"Glass and steel aren't all that bad, you know." Ryan took another step.

"If used sparingly."

"If used artistically." He was right in front of her.

"Sparingly artistic."

"Artistically sparing." Ryan reached for her face.

With a gentle, feathery touch, the back of his knuckles brushed her cheek. Tamsyn felt it deeply in her chest, and her eyes widened at her own reaction.

The teakettle whistled and broke her muse.

CHAPTER SIXTEEN

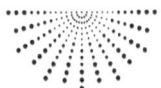

"*H*ave you ever photographed this entire house?" Ryan asked as he sat down on the rocking chair on the side porch overlooking a garden of roses, gardenias, azaleas, and lilies.

The chair rocked, and his cup of hot Darjeeling sloshed about in the dainty teacup, but he managed to catch the tea on an equally dainty saucer.

"I took some photos of the house, yes." Tamsyn placed the teapot on the side table that separated Ryan's chair from hers.

"I mean a professional photographer. I have a friend who does this for a living. I'll call him. See when he could come here to—"

"How much would it cost?" Tamsyn asked.

"Don't worry about it. It's on me."

"Why?"

"Because I want to help you preserve this house. Lots of memories here, you said."

Tamsyn eyed him with what looked like suspicious brows. "Why?"

"Because I lo—uh, I'm doing you a favor." He sipped his tea, trying to shut up.

"A favor? After the photography is done, the house is gone?"

"If you sell it. If you don't, then it's a new day. What if you found some investors willing to help you save the house?"

"I tried. Save Old Savannah failed before it even really took off."

"Ah. So that was what SOS was for." A tiny horn sounded, and Ryan's eyes went to the source. It was a little car going down Rosa Pendegrast Lane.

"Back in the old days, we'd be watching horse-drawn carriages instead of putt-putt cars," Tamsyn said.

"Oh boy. Can you imagine the smell of horses?"

Tamsyn gave him a look. "You're no fun."

Ryan knew she was joking. "Must be nice to have your last name on a street sign."

Tamsyn shrugged. "Doesn't bother me."

"Thank you for the tour. That was enlightening."

"My pleasure."

"Seems to me that your mother did a lot of work preserving the history of the house."

"Yes."

"Even though it's Rosa Pendegrast Lane over there, the house and garden are here today because of Caleigh Pendegrast."

Tamsyn nodded.

Ryan wasn't sure, but he thought he saw tears pool in her eyes.

"Mom did an enormous amount of work trying to get back some of the furniture that my relatives carted off after my grandfather passed away. She spent a fortune. Dad let her do whatever it took to preserve the family heirlooms."

She sighed so loudly that Ryan was startled.

"And here I am. I've failed my mother, my grandfather, my great-grandmother, and whoever else up the family tree had something to do with this house."

"Failed? Failed is a strong word, Tamsyn." Ryan wanted to reach for her hand, but the teapot and the side table blocked his access to her.

They sat in silence for a while, sipping Darjeeling.

"You know, you won't part with this house, because your mother put so much of her life into it," Ryan finally said.

"She did. This garden is—was—hers as well."

"You feel that if you let go of this house, you'll let go of your mother's memories."

"I don't want to forget Mom."

"You won't. Aren't you supposed to write a book or something?"

Tamsyn didn't reply.

"You haven't written it because you didn't want to revisit the difficult days of losing your mother."

"She died of cancer," Tamsyn said quietly. "It's been tough for Dad."

"And you. Talking about your mother might help you with your grief."

"Does it?"

"How about this? Why don't you tell me, and I'll write it down for you?" Ryan wasn't sure how that idea popped into his head, but he could take dictation, especially if it meant spending more time with Tamsyn.

"You?"

"Are you insulting me?" Ryan asked. "Just because I flunked history in college doesn't mean I can't string two sentences together."

"If you string two sentences together, that's called a run-on sentence."

"Har, har." Ryan drank more tea as he processed what she had just said.

Silence again.

Ryan thought of something else. "I could help you with the architecture of this house."

"You don't care about the past."

"I do care about architecture."

"Great. An architectural paper with human footnotes."

"Or human appendices."

"You crack me up. If Mom heard us—"

She clammed up.

"God called her home to heaven," Ryan said.

"She'll never see me get married. She'll never babysit my children."

Get married.

Have children.

Never before had those phrases affected Ryan as they did at this moment, this early May afternoon, warm and muggy in the low seventies as they drank...hot tea!

What is wrong with us?

"Why are we drinking hot tea?" Ryan asked.

"I drink hot tea year round. I drink ice tea at Piper's Place or other restaurants, but rarely at home."

"Okay. For a moment there, I thought we were in love."

"With tea?" Tamsyn asked.

"You know how falling in love can make you do irrational things."

Tamsyn laughed so loudly her teacup and saucer rattled against each other. "It's never irrational to drink hot tea in the summer in the South. Where are you from, anyway?"

"Georgia. I'm a native."

"Then you should know we do things like drink hot tea in the summer and eat fried ice cream."

"Yeah. Well, my family is nontraditional in many ways. We don't drink much tea since Mother —Anyway, I never had a hankering for fried ice cream. I prefer sushi."

Tamsyn's eyes softened. "I'm okay with sushi, but Mom loved it. We'd sit on Dad's riverboat and eat sushi for dinner at least once a week. Dad didn't care for it at all. He's a hamburger guy."

"Ah, we're going to get along, your dad and I."

"I think Mom would've loved to meet you too..."

Tamsyn's voice trailing off broke Ryan's heart.

He wasn't sure what to do.

Tamsyn closed her eyes. She rocked in her rocking chair. "Mom and I used to sit out here, drink tea, talk about antiques and which parts of the house she was going to restore next. It was a costly hobby, but Dad didn't mind as long as Mom was happy. Then the cancer..."

Her voice trailed off again.

Again!

Ryan couldn't bear it.

Ryan put down his cup and saucer on the side table. He took Tamsyn's cup away from her and neatly set it next to his.

He pulled her to her feet, wrapped his warm arms around Tamsyn's waist, and drew her close, forehead to forehead.

"I've had a wonderful week with you, Tamsyn. Best vacation ever."

"But now you must go back to work."

"Monday. My two business partners are taking care of business this week. Well, Hiroki is holding up the fort, and Jared is giving him fits. That's the way it rolls at RYUCP."

"It's hard when you have a business partnership. That's why I'm the sole owner of Tamsyn Tours."

"Your dad's not involved?"

"We split the riverboat cruise profits, but that's about it."

"Why are we talking about business?" Ryan asked.

"You started it."

"I was talking about doing irrational things out of love."

"If your love comes from God, it's very rational. God is love, and there is no other type of love worthy of being called such."

"You just said *love* three times in that statement," Ryan said.

"Meaning what?"

"It's on your mind."

"And yours." Tamsyn's voice was whisper soft.

"Yes..." His lips found hers, softly at first, and then with a determination he didn't know he had.

Ryan knew then that he didn't want to let Tamsyn go.

CHAPTER SEVENTEEN

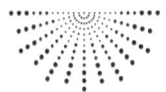

*B*ut let her go he must.

Work beckoned, and by Monday morning at eight on the dot, Ryan Ruttledge was home in Atlanta, back at the glass desk in his sterile executive office—steel, crystal, and all. The air conditioner blasted all around him, making his heart feel colder by the minute.

Hiroki was silent as he sat on the other side of the table, swiping his iPad, ignoring Ryan for the most part.

"What?" Ryan asked between sips of cappuccino.

Silence.

"What, Hiroki?"

A grunt. Then Hiroki let it out. "Here's the

deal. We sent you to Savannah on a scouting mission."

"Yeah. I'd say it was a success."

"No, it wasn't. You were supposed to figure out how the opposition thinks and how we could knock down Save Old Savannah. You weren't supposed to fall in love with the city."

I didn't fall in love with the city.

I fell in love with—

Wow. I did, didn't I?

"Life happens." It was all Ryan wanted to say.

"Life didn't just happen, Ryan, old boy." Hiroki tapped his iPad something fierce. "Have you even prayed about this?"

"Some."

"Pray more. It's entirely possible you were seduced."

"And that would be your fault." Ryan pointed at Hiroki. "You put me up to it with the double tickets to the Friday night romantic riverboat cruise."

"My mistake."

The door opened, and in walked Jared Urquhart. He went straight to the cappuccino machine. "I see you've already started fighting without me."

Hiroki grunted. "Tell him, Ryan."

"Tell me what?" Jared asked.

"He's in love."

"Can't help you there." Jared laughed. He plopped down on a sofa nearby and savored his cappuccino. He glanced at Ryan, then at Hiroki. "Maybe I don't want to know."

"Yes, you do, Jared. The woman is Tamsyn Pendegrast, whose Queen Anne Victorian we're trying to buy for the project in Savannah."

"That's good, isn't it?" Jared glanced at Ryan. "Now you can persuade her to give it up."

"That's the problem," Hiroki said. "Ryan now believes the Victorian needs to be preserved."

Ryan cleared his throat. "I've been looking at other options. Just four blocks south of there are some vacant lots and rundown office complexes we can buy. Down the road from River Street, near the Talmadge Memorial Bridge, there are some warehouses we can convert into mixed-use complexes. We don't need Rosa Pendegrast Lane."

"What are we going to do with the two houses we've already bought?" Jared asked.

"Glad you asked." Ryan leaned forward at his desk. "I found two more nineteenth-century houses for sale a block or so away. What if we take those four houses and turn them into a living museum as part of our mixed-use plan?"

Jared appeared intrigued.

Ryan waited.

"You mean fix them up to be period-authentic

and then..." Jared asked.

"And then rent them out to people who want to live in historic homes but don't want to mess with their high maintenance."

"Vacationers?"

"Anyone." *Like me, for example. If I move to Savannah, I could rent one of these houses.* Ryan decided he'd talk to Jared later about opening an RYUCP branch in Savannah. "It's nothing new, Jared. There are historic homes in Savannah for rent."

"Sure."

"And you can go to France and rent a historic chateau, for example."

"Right, but these are no chateaus or castles," Jared reminded him.

"Savannah might be smaller, but the potential is there. You can rent a small nineteenth-century historic home for six or seven hundred a night. I think for these houses, we could go for more. And if we wanted to sell—let's say, down the road—historic homes have high property values in that city."

"There's that." Jared nodded. "Still, if the two *new* properties you found are anything like the two we've already bought to demolish, the costs of recon- struction would be enormous."

"We could get an estimate from Brooks Reno. You know they'll give us a fair price."

"True. Have you talked to Brinley Brooks?" Jared asked.

Yes, Ryan had. Brinley Books ran Brooks Renovations out of St. Simon's Island, but the company worked up and down the coast, from Savannah to Darien to St. Mary's and beyond. Ryan had thought of Brooks Renovations because it had a good reputation, and Jared had known Brinley since they were kids living next door to each other on Sea Island.

Still, Ryan wanted to clear the air so Jared didn't misunderstand that Ryan hadn't overstepped his position as vice president. "I didn't call Brinley about our properties. I called her about Tam's house."

"So it's Tam now, huh?" Jared put his cup on the glass coffee table in front of him.

"I wanted to know how much it would cost to fix up Tam's 1882 house. I figured if I sold some stocks, I could help her out."

"Okay. That's a private matter." Jared leaned back on the couch. "Tell me, Ryan. Who's going to manage the living museum?"

"I'm thinking that since we already have properties in Savannah, we should have an RYUCP office there."

Jared grinned. "Your office."

Hiroki shook his head. "Can't fight love."

"How much are those two other houses?" Jared

asked.

"Glad you asked. I called Dominic. He said one of the houses is underpriced and the current homeowners have restored the first floor. They ran out of money. Divorce scenario."

"As long as we don't spend more than two mil per house, does that sound okay to you, Hiroki?" Jared rubbed his temples and cringed.

Ryan wondered if Jared was nursing another hangover. Someday, when he had a good opportunity—and enough guts—he would witness to Jared, tell him about Jesus, the curer of the ills in his heart. Jared didn't need all those spirits from bars if he had the Holy Spirit of God.

Then again, to each his own. Ryan could tell Jared about Jesus, but Jared had to make his own decision.

Meanwhile, Ryan had some historic homes to salvage.

"So now we're no longer demolishing, but we're preserving history?" Hiroki asked. His voice sounded amused, but at the same time his face looked pleased. Ryan couldn't interpret that mixed reaction.

Jared turned his attention to Hiroki. "Seriously, what do you think?"

Hiroki drew a deep breath.

"Can't fight love," he said again.

CHAPTER EIGHTEEN

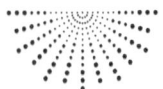

The long-distance relationship had taken a toll on both of them, especially on Tamsyn. Every Friday evening in May and June, Ryan had flown into Savannah, and every late Sunday night or early Monday morning, he had flown back to Atlanta.

All that flying back and forth meant too many goodbyes for Tamsyn to bear.

Every weekend, Ryan stayed for two or three nights on the *Caleigh Pendegrast* riverboat, which made her dad terribly happy to have someone to beat at chess.

Yes, it had surprised Tamsyn that Ryan played chess.

It had surprised her even more that Ryan had chosen to spend his weekends in Savannah with her, working around her Saturday tour schedules, attending Riverside Chapel with her, and hanging out with her friends from church.

And her dad.

How long could this last?

This Sunday, after the evening service, Tamsyn decided they needed to talk about it. Ryan would have to be out the door by four in the morning to catch his five-thirty Monday morning flight back to Atlanta and get back to work.

Piper's Place was never empty. It was close to ten o'clock, and they were sitting by the window on the third floor, looking at the night lights up and down Savannah River and eating peach cobbler after their seafood dinner.

"Something's on your mind," Ryan said quietly.

"Thank you for the Brooks Reno appraisal," Tamsyn began tentatively.

"Uh-oh. Is there a problem?"

"This is the seventh weekend in a row you've spent in Savannah." She didn't want to hurt Ryan's feelings, but it needed to be said.

"With you."

"It's not practical."

"I don't care about the money."

"I can see that."

"I'm racking up frequent flyer miles." Ryan reached across the table for Tamsyn's hand.

"Besides, the flight is only one hour each way. It beats driving five hours here and five hours back."

"For five hundred dollars each round trip."

"It's worth it. You're worth it. You're priceless to me."

She let him massage the back of her hand. That was nice, but it only happened on weekends. The rest of the week, she was alone, and so was he.

"I can't move to Atlanta," Tamsyn confessed. "There, I said it."

"And I can't move to Savannah. I want to, but my job is in Atlanta."

"Mine is in Savannah. I can't give Savannah tours in Atlanta." She laughed.

"I'm more flexible than you. I'm going to talk to my partners about opening an RYUCP branch in Savannah. It could take a few years."

Years? Yikes. "Meanwhile, you keep buying plane tickets? It just feels like a waste of money."

"Nothing I do for you is a waste of money or time."

"That's endearing, Ryan."

"Endearing? That's all?"

"You know me. I'm a practical person. Two thousand dollars of plane tickets a month times twelve adds up. That's practically a year's salary for some people."

Ryan retracted his hand from Tamsyn's.

His face steeled.

He finished his peach cobbler without another word.

"I'm sorry." Tamsyn really was. "I prayed about it, but I don't see how we can work out."

"You *prayed* about it? Well, I did too."

"Good. What did God say to you?" Tamsyn tried to keep it cheerful, but she knew what Ryan was getting at.

Don't use the God card to justify her own rationale.

Well, it's logical for him to save his money. Twenty-four thousand dollars a year of plane tickets.

"What about the discussions on restoring your house?" Ryan asked.

"Thank you—again—for paying for the appraisal that Brooks Renovations did, but the price is too steep, and I can't afford it at this time, even with your offer to pay for half of it."

"I'll pay for all of it," Ryan said.

"I don't want you to go into debt."

"For you, I'll do anything."

"If you go into debt, you're going have a heap of financial trouble, and that's going to destroy our relationship."

"Seriously?" Ryan put down his fork. In spite of their fractious conversation, Tamsyn noted that he had polished off his peach cobbler.

"Seems like you've been negative all evening," Ryan said.

"I'm trying to be prac—"

"Yeah, yeah. Want to hear what I think?"

"S-sure."

"Tamsyn, I think you're afraid."

"Afraid? I'm not afraid." Only then did Tamsyn realize that her hand was shaking as it reached for her glass of cold water with lime in it.

"Let me finish, will you?" Ryan leaned forward.

His brown eyes met hers. For a moment, Tamsyn forgot why she had to stand her ground, why she had to do what she had to do, why she had to—whatever it was.

"What are you working for, Tamsyn Pendegrast? In ten, twenty years, will Tamsyn Tours be all there is to life?"

"Not life, but livelihood. It's my job."

"I hear you. You love giving tours. You love this city. But this city, your career, your tours—none of those things are your life."

"No, of course not. I have God."

"Exactly. And what does God tell you about your life?"

"I want to serve Him, do some church work, go on mission trips. I can't do any of that if I don't have the money, you know. I feel that Tamsyn Tours gives me a vehicle to be able to give to the church and help its ministries."

"That's a noble cause. You know that I tithe too, right? At Midtown Chapel, I sponsor mission trips and inner-city kids attending VBS and teen camps."

I didn't know that. "That's good."

"But I want a family too."

Tamsyn didn't know what to say about that.

"You're turning twenty-eight soon. Have you thought about getting married, having kids?" Ryan asked.

"Not now."

"I'm talking about you and me. Marry me, Tamsyn."

What! "Did you just propose to me?"

"I guess I did. Oh, I don't have a ring. But I am serious about this."

"You've been thinking about it?"

"I have. I don't want to lose you, Tam."

"See what I mean? Weren't we talking about this very thing? We can't just do *whatever.*"

"We're not doing *whatever.*"

"We can't be a part-time couple, seeing each other only on weekends. It won't work for me."

"Then move to Atlanta."

"We've also discussed that only minutes ago, Ryan."

"I'll find a way to move to Savannah, then."

"In a few years, you said."

"Well, until then..."

"Maybe you could look me up in a few years."

"What are you saying?" Ryan's face looked stunned.

"Maybe this isn't working out."

"We should pray about this before we call it quits."

"I don't know how it'll work out."

"God knows," Ryan said. "Nothing is impossible with Him. Romans 8:28."

"That's another verse, Ryan. Luke 1:37 says, 'For with God nothing will be impossible.' Is that what you had in mind?"

"I was thinking of another verse similar to that." Ryan produced his iPhone and looked it up. "Here it is. Mark 10:27."

> *But Jesus looked at them and said, "With men it is impossible, but not with God; for with God all things are possible."*

"Of course, you know what Romans 8:28 says."

> *And we know that all things work together for good to those who love God, to those who are the called according to His purpose.*

"There you go," Ryan said. "Maybe we should both keep that in mind."

"And until we know what God's will is for us, don't spend any more money on plane tickets coming to Savannah," Tamsyn replied. "Agreed?"

"I have to see you."

"I'll miss you too."

"But?"

"We have to know if our feelings are simply emotional reactions to each other, irrational things we do when we're in love. Do you remember saying that when we had tea on my back porch?"

Ryan nodded. "I enjoyed that. I want to have tea with you every afternoon the rest of my life."

"If it's God's will for us, then we will, but we have to be sure, right?" Tamsyn asked.

"Which leads us back to the *impossible* verses," Ryan said. "I think we should remember one more verse, Tam. Maybe this is what we should pray over."

"That is?"

"Hebrews 11:6."

But without faith it is impossible to please Him, for he who comes to God must believe that He is, and that He is a rewarder of those who diligently seek Him.

"That's my mom's favorite verse," Tamsyn said.

"Was it?"

Tamsyn nodded. Eyes closed, she held back tears.

A warm arm went around her shoulders. She didn't have to look up. It was Ryan. As quick as lightning, he had slid out of his seat across the table and sat down next to her.

He said nothing as he wiped tears from Tamsyn's eyes with a napkin—a coarse napkin!

She didn't complain.

"I'm in love with you," Ryan whispered in her ear. "I will always love you, even if you can't see us being together."

CHAPTER NINETEEN

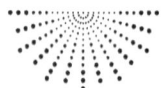

*F*ourth of July was a lucrative time of year for Tamsyn Tours. It had begun on the third of July with fireworks on Tybee Island, and ended on the evening of the Fourth with Tamsyn and her tour guides dropping off the tourists at River Street where they would go for dinner—twenty percent discount at Piper's Place and other local eateries—followed by fireworks over Savannah River.

Tamsyn could've had dinner and watched fireworks with Dad on his special Independence Day dinner cruise, but she was exhausted. All she wanted to do was to go home and get some rest. If she had any energy left, she might check her emails, work on her company finances, and then go to bed.

She parked her car on Rosa Pendegrast Lane,

hauled her tote bag and backpack out of the trunk, and trekked up the sidewalk to her house. She wondered if someday she might own a house with a garage. If she did, she wanted carriage doors. Until then, here she was, parking her car on the roadside.

It wasn't raining tonight. It hadn't rained for a couple of weeks in Savannah. Clear weather was always good for tourism. Rain didn't go well with walking tours or fireworks or riverboat cruises. And rain didn't go well with her carrying all her stuff from the car to the house.

She bolted the front door behind her in the foyer, and stared up the steep stairs.

Her calves hurt. Her heels also hurt. In spite of her hiking boots and the sole pads, her plantar fasciitis on her left foot was acting up again. She was worn out, but she didn't feel like climbing up those stairs to her bedroom.

She dragged her bags to the sitting room and plopped down on the sofa. This was Mom's favorite sofa, and she particularly liked the Aubusson tapestry.

Tamsyn kicked off her boots, rubbed her heels, and stretched out on the sofa. She closed her eyes.

A little tune came from her iPhone.

"Leave me alone, will you!" Tamsyn mumbled as she reached for her tote bag.

It was Dad, learning to text.

Tamsyn waded through the typos and concluded that Dad just wanted to say hello.

She texted back.

Don't stay up too late.

She rolled back onto the sofa. She thought she should get up and make herself some dinner. She probably had one frozen chicken pot pie left she could microwave.

She should wind down and then go to bed.

She didn't feel like working on her finances or watching TV.

Tamsyn had never been one to watch television. She was more like Mom, who had preferred books to video. TV was Dad's thing. He could sit in front of the TV all day long if there wasn't any work to be done.

Tamsyn could see them now in this sitting room, which hadn't changed in decades. Mom would be busy looking at swatches and upholstery designs while Dad watched football, oblivious to the escalating costs incurred in keeping an old house period authentic.

Still, those were the days when they had been a happy family.

After having had several miscarriages after Tamsyn, Mom and Dad had adopted a baby girl so that Tamsyn could have a sibling. It hadn't worked out. When Bernadette had turned eighteen, she left the Pendegrast family and was never seen again. Her last words—in a scrawled letter—had declared that she hated them all and wanted to be liberated.

Sometimes Tamsyn wondered what happened to Bernadette, whether she knew that Mom had passed away from cancer and that Dad now lived on the riverboat, where Bernadette had loved to play as a child.

The grandfather clock ticked loudly in Tamsyn's ears, but she had heard it so many times in her life that it was just background noise now.

Soon, she was thinking of Mom's restoration projects and wondering whether she should try to finish restoring that one room upstairs, Tamsyn's own bedroom. Mom had said that she had left that room for Tamsyn to fix up.

Tamsyn knew that Mom had said that only because her bedroom was too messy.

Mom didn't like messes.

She liked everything just so. Neat and tidy, and everything in place.

That was how the Pendegrast family home had been preserved.

In the end, when Mom had been diagnosed with lung cancer—oddly enough, she never smoked —Dad had taken over, keeping the house the way Mom liked it: untouched.

After Mom had passed away, Dad decided to

renovate the kitchen. It was the only place in the entire house that he felt Mom would be fine with if he updated it.

Hiring a local contractor whose business was to restore historic homes, Dad had the kitchen gutted. He replaced the floor, cabinets, sinks, refrigerator, stove, and just about everything in the kitchen. Due to Dad's indecision about countertops and back-splash color selection, the renovation went on for weeks.

And weeks.

Tamsyn could hear the construction noise now. It was loud, and it—

Crackled and popped?

And roared?

And smelled like—

Smoke!

Tamsyn sprang off the sofa. The strong smoky smell came from everywhere. At first she thought her fireplace—

No. It was outside.

She peeked out the window.

The sky above Rosa Pendegrast Lane was gray and hazy in the streetlights. There was some-thing yellowish and orangey coming from her backyard.

Oh no.

Barefoot, she grabbed her iPhone from the

coffee table and ran to her front door and down the sidewalk. She spun around—

That was when she saw it.

Her neighbor's 1854 gingerbread house on the other side of Tamsyn's magnolia tree was engulfed in flames, only yards away from her house. As she stood there, an explosion lifted part of the roof off the burning house, spraying splintered wood and flares of fire every which way.

Tamsyn dropped on her hands and knees. She looked up.

What was that?

She gasped as flares of fire jumped through her magnolia tree and onto her back porch, setting her roof and porch planks on fire!

Oh no!

"Lord, help us!" She dialed 911 and found out they had already received several calls.

She wondered whether to go back to her house to pick up a few things—

She got on her feet and turned to run back into her house—

"Miss Tam, no!"

Someone grabbed her arms.

"Mom's Bible," Tamsyn replied, but it was more than that. Mom's books, bookshelves, furniture, fireplace, wallpaper, Mom's life's work!

Must salvage something!

"No, Miss Tam!" One of her neighbor's sons—who lived on the other side of Rosa Pendegrast Lane —stood in front of her. The other two ushered her away from her house and down the stone path to the sidewalk.

"It's safer on the other side of the street. Let's get her there. She looks shocked."

Shocked? Me?

"Where's the fire truck? Where are they?" Tamsyn shouted, her voice floating in the air in a surreal time lapse.

Mom had poured her life into that house. If the house went, Mom's memories...

Mom's memories would be gone!

Then she heard the sirens.

CHAPTER TWENTY

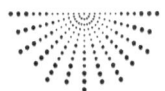

*R*yan had chosen not to play golf with his father this morning. He couldn't imagine spending five days a week on the golf course when he could be working and earning income. One day off for Independence Day had been enough, hadn't it?

Well, he had to give it to Ryan Ruttledge IV. Dad had worked hard all his life, and now he deserved to enjoy the fruit of his success: retirement.

Ryan wasn't there yet.

Nope.

An early riser—like Tamsyn—Ryan was in his empty Buckhead office by five o'clock. The RYUCP employees had had a rousing Fourth of July celebration the night before, and Ryan doubted any one of them would be arriving at work early this morning.

Ryan was hoping for a quiet place to work to get his mind off Tamsyn. He would have until about nine o'clock, when office hours began.

Seriously, four hours weren't enough to make him forget Tamsyn.

Eleven days and counting.

Eleven days without any communication with Tamsyn. No emails. No texts. No phone calls.

No more euphonious voice.

He missed her. He wished they could have worked out something, but she was right.

Two hundred and fifty miles between them did not a relationship make.

His only recourse, like hers, was to immerse himself in work. So here he was, at the RYUCP glass tower.

Alone.

He was drinking his third cup of coffee, when Hiroki called from his house in Alpharetta.

Ryan picked up his office phone. "Morning."

"What's wrong with your iPhone?" Hiroki snapped.

"I forgot it this morning. Left it at home. I'll pick it up at lunchtime. I'm not expecting any personal calls. Why?"

"Did you see the news?" Hiroki asked. "Six o'clock."

"What? It's already six o'clock?" Ryan couldn't

recall what he had been doing for an hour in his office.

"It's 6:12, Ryan."

Ryan groaned. Sometimes he didn't know what to do with Hiroki. "Do I look like a person who watches the news?"

"I figured. I'm emailing you several news clips in chronological order."

"About another animal-rescue success story?" Ryan laughed. Hiroki had a soft spot for animals, judging by his Facebook posts and his emails to his friends.

Ryan couldn't imagine owning any pet, but Hiroki had eight dogs he had rescued from the pound. Hiroki was looking for a bigger house to buy so he could rescue more Labs and golden retrievers.

"No, you will want to see this piece of news. I can't get hold of Jared, but I'll send him a copy too. Emailing you now. Got it?"

"Let me check." Ryan cleared his screen and logged into his email account. There were several emails there that he hadn't read this morning—only because this was the first time today he'd checked his email. One from Dominic Khan, RYUCP's Savannah real estate agent, marked urgent.

Hiroki's email had an empty subject line. Just like him not to title his emails.

Ryan decided he'd humor his friend. He clicked on the morning news link from—

Savannah?

"What's up, Hiroki?" Ryan asked as the reporter's face filled the screen.

"It happened in the wee hours of the morning," Hiroki said. "Put me on the speakerphone."

Ryan did. "Did you say this morning?"

"Between midnight and one o'clock."

"Five or six hours ago..." Ryan turned up the volume on his computer monitor.

"Firefighters have arrived and are busy putting out the fire." The reporter stood on a street corner. Behind her, fire trucks and SCMPD vehicles dotted the small street. Beside her, curious onlookers were staring into the local TV camera. Above her, the street sign said Rosa Pendegrast Lane.

No!

"Tamsyn!" Ryan jumped out of his chair.

"She's okay," Hiroki said.

"You sure?"

"Yeah. I just called Pastor Flores of Riverside Chapel—he was already up—and he said Tamsyn is okay," Hiroki explained. "If you'd checked your email sooner or had your iPhone with you, you would have known this."

"My iPhone was recharging in my home office.

That's how I left home without it... Wait a sec. Did you say you called Pastor Flores?"

"To find out if Tamsyn is okay."

"Why would he talk to you? Does he know you? Why would he tell you anything about Tamsyn?"

"I said that I was calling on behalf of my idiot friend who is concerned—or should be concerned—about his girlfriend but is afraid—or would be afraid—to ask."

"You what?!"

"Your girlfriend was in danger, and where were you? In your own little bubble."

"I'm at work, Hiroki. Besides, she's not my girlfriend anymore. We parted ways."

"How poetic, Ryan."

"Shut up and let me watch the rest of this." He shook his head. "Whew. Thank God Tam is okay."

Thank You, Lord!

The reporter stood among three boys who dwarfed her. "We're here with three teenagers, the heroes of the night. What can you tell us, Adrian?"

"We were up late playing Wii at Hector's house across the street. Our windows were open, and we smelled and heard the fire. We called 911 and then went outside to see what's going on, you know."

"And then?"

"We saw that other house on fire, and so we knocked on the neighbors' doors to tell them to get out. We were coming up to Miss Tam's house when she came outside just before the other house's roof blew off."

Miss Tam.

Tamsyn!

Ryan was on his feet again. He put his palms on the table, leaning down with his eyes on the screen. "And I wasn't there for her."

The reporter wasn't finished. "Then?"

"She wanted to go back inside to get her mama's Bible, but we stopped her."

"Yeah," his friend said. "She's a nice lady and all, but she was screaming her head off. It took three of us to pin her down so she didn't go back in—"

"That was something else!" the third kid said. "I can't believe Miss Tam wanted to risk her life for a book—"

"It's the Bible," the kid named Hector nudged his friend.

"Everybody knows they can reprint a Bible. You can even get it online for free."

It has to be more than that.

Tamsyn probably thought that she had time.

Ryan felt sick.

He stopped the video clip.

"I have to fly to Savannah," Ryan said.

"There are several flights out this morning—I

checked. Want me to pick you up from the office?" Hiroki asked.

"Thanks, friend, but I'll just drive to the airport. It'll take you longer to get here than I can get to the airport."

"Make it an off-site workday. Or better yet, take the rest of the week off, if you have to. Jared will understand."

Oh yeah. It was only Thursday. Then again, it might be a waste of effort.

"I don't think Tamsyn wants me around, frankly. I'll just go see how she is doing, and then I'll fly home tonight."

"Whatever suits you, man."

"Hiroki?"

"Yeah?"

"Will you pray for me and Tam? I want God's will for us, but it's killing me to be away from her this long. I was willing to accept seeing her only two days a week, but it's been eleven days."

"I'll pray for you. You know something? Soldiers who get deployed are separated from their loved ones for more than eleven days. They endure it."

"They know they have someone to come home to."

"Good point. In your case, maybe we should pray for you to have faith in God."

Faith. What I need.

That reminded Ryan of his last conversation with Tamsyn. He had shared a verse about faith with her, and she had said it was her mom's favorite verse. Hebrews 11:6.

> *But without faith it is impossible to please Him, for he who comes to God must believe that He is, and that He is a rewarder of those who diligently seek Him.*

"What if it's not God's will for us to be together again?"

"Then you won't," Hiroki said. "Meanwhile, we have a problem. When you get to Savannah, survey the damages. I've already made arrangements for Dominic to get an appraisal. The insurance could pay for a complete restoration. This could move your living museum idea forward faster than we expected."

Insurance.

"And the same for Tam's house, then," Ryan said.

"Probably. It wasn't her fault the house burned down. It's under investigation, I'm sure. I wouldn't be surprised if there were some illegal fireworks happening, with it being Independence Day and all."

"I'll touch base with Dominic and see what he

says. Bet he didn't realize that handling our properties could be this messy."

"What properties? One of them is totally burned to the ground, and the other has water damage on every floor. Water, you know, is the enemy of historic homes."

"And how did you suddenly know so much about historic homes?" Ryan asked.

"Just talked to Dominic. He's like a walking search engine of historic homes in Savannah. We should hire him to be part of our Savannah office. And his daughter is kinda cute."

"Dominic has a daughter? He doesn't look old enough to be... Where are we going with this, Hiroki?"

"I'm thinking I need to make a trip to Savannah too."

Ryan chuckled. "I'll pray for you, man. Whoever you date has to put up with your idiosyncrasies."

"You mean my eye for detail?"

"That too. You do keep up with things. And you've come to my aid so many times, Hiroki. For that, I appreciate you. Thank you for telling me about this fire, and I'm going to let you go now so I can buy a plane ticket."

"Sounds good."

"Hey, Hiroki?"

"Yeah?"

"You're a good friend. Now go back to sleep. You're going to have to be here at nine to fill in for Jared and me."

"I drank too much coffee to go back to bed. So excited for you, Ryan."

Excited? "About what?"

"Just remember I'm your best man."

Best man? Ryan wasn't sure what Hiroki meant, but he had already hung up. Did he mean he wanted to be Ryan's best man at his wedding?

Wedding?

What wedding?

To have a wedding he'd need a bride.

She's reluctant.

She has a hang-up of some sort.

"Lord Jesus, whatever it is that Tam is going through, give her strength to prevail. Fill her life with love—mine, I hope, not some other guy's—and most importantly, fill her heart with Your love, Lord. Of course."

Ryan bought the first ticket he could get on the Delta Airlines website.

He was driving down Interstate 85 before he realized he had to go home to pick up his iPhone. He had barely enough time to get to the airport with this detour.

He floored the gas pedal.

CHAPTER TWENTY-ONE

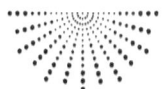

"*I*t's all my fault." Tamsyn's shoulders sagged as her new boots stomped the ashen heap that was once Mom's precious library. She was surrounded by partially collapsed blackened brick walls. It was obvious which parts of the Queen Anne house were built of brick and which parts were all wood. The wood had been consumed by the fire in the night.

Tamsyn looked for that old family Bible, but not a single book remained.

Mom's Bible is gone.

The fire had spread quickly, consumed anything paper, wood, cloth, and combustible, and had left only the lower foundations standing.

From where Tamsyn stood, she could see clear through to the backyard where the magnolia tree had been burned down to a stump. Dad stomped across the wet grass toward her. The ground had been saturated with water from the fire hoses hours before.

"It's not your fault, honey." Dad combed through the rubble with a stick he had found.

He must have heard her talking aloud to herself.

Car doors closed behind her, and Tamsyn turned to look.

Pastor Flores and Heidi waved to them. Heidi reached Tamsyn first with a sisterly hug that said it all. Riverside Chapel would support her and help her in any way in her recovery.

A few steps away, Pastor Flores shook hands with Dad.

"How are you?" Heidi asked Tamsyn.

"I'll be okay."

Tamsyn remembered her visit to Heidi's house about two months ago when she had found out that her last two neighbors had sold their historic homes to Ruttledge Yamada Urquhart Commercial Properties. She remembered how she and Heidi had prayed, and she had—for some reason she was beginning to understand now—surrendered her house to God.

Thank You, Lord, for loving me. You're all I need.

Take my house, if You so choose, Lord. I give it to You.

And yes, God had taken it.

"My neighbors told me the arson investigators were here this morning." Tamsyn pointed to one of the destroyed houses. "They spent a lot of time over there."

Heidi nodded. "This house is insured, right?"

"Yeah, we have some ultra expensive coverage because it's a historic home."

"Good for you. They'll pay for the restoration down to the crown moldings."

"The bad news is I lost a lot of things from my family," Tamsyn said.

"And the good news?" Heidi asked.

"About a month ago, Brooks Renovations gave me a quote on how much it would cost to restore it."

"How did you decide to do that? You didn't tell me about it."

"I've been so busy—sorry. Besides, it was Ryan's idea. He paid for the private appraisal because he wanted to be a part of the restoration. Only our relationship didn't go that far, and that was the end of it."

"God worked it all out, didn't He?" Heidi asked. "Romans 8:28."

"Ryan mentioned that verse too. I just don't see how it applies here though."

Heidi smiled. "The way I see it, God knows the future. The appraisal helps your insurance claims."

"Ah, yes."

"And they took pictures."

"Yes, they did. I thought it was odd, but Brooks Reno sent a professional antique appraiser, some friend of Brinley Brooks, and he took all sorts of photographs. In fact, I have a DVD of the tour. He made a documentary of this house."

"There you go. Romans 8:28," Heidi reminded her.

"But Mom's Bible is gone." Tamsyn sobbed quietly.

Heidi hugged her. "We have Jesus in our hearts. He is the Word of God. We can find another Bible of the same period and era."

"It won't have Mom's handwritten notes in it."

"She is in heaven, and you'll see her again. That's more valuable."

"I agree. Sorry I'm so silly."

"No, no. You're not. You're grieving."

"It's just a house fire." Tamsyn shrugged. "Dad's alive. I'm alive. It is well with our souls."

"When I said grieving, I meant you're still grieving your mom," Heidi explained.

"How can that be? She's been gone eight years." *Actually, almost nine, give or take a few weeks.*

"They say daughters sometimes grieve their moms for longer periods of time."

Tamsyn couldn't agree more. She blinked away

sorrow of things gone and lost, of memories ebbing into the passage of time. Of Mom's smiles, Mom's touch, Mom's hugs.

I so miss Mom's hugs.

I miss her saying that she loves me.

And that everything is going to be okay in the Lord.

Another vehicle door slammed behind Tamsyn.

She heard footsteps coming up the brick path.

Familiar footsteps.

CHAPTER TWENTY-TWO

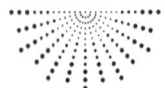

*R*yan looked around the property. Wow. The damage was extensive. They'd have to rebuild the entire building from the foundation up. Those burned brick walls looked like they could collapse any day.

He watched as Pastor Flores and Heidi waved to him, then joined Tamsyn's dad to scour the rubble, away from where Tamsyn was standing.

Tamsyn was looking directly at him.

"Why are you here?" She glared.

"Same reason you're here." Ryan didn't step any closer. Not wanting to push Tamsyn away, he waited for her to make the first move. Sure, it had been only ten days since he last saw her, but it had felt like a lifetime.

Well, he had already made the first move by flying into Savannah and driving here to find her.

And he supposed Tamsyn's dad had approved the move since he was the one who had replied to his text regarding their whereabouts. Ryan had a feeling that Jerome Pendegrast knew his daughter needed a friend—or someone more than a friend.

He stood there and waited for Tamsyn to say something else.

"I've lost the house." Tamsyn's voice was barely audible.

"Perhaps, in its original condition." Ryan's hands dug into his jean pockets. "We will rebuild."

He realized he had said *we*, but he wasn't going to retract it.

"It won't be the same." If there was a way to describe her voice as *crestfallen*, this was it.

"It will be a replica of the original."

"It's not the original."

Ryan wasn't sure how to counter that. "You and I are the originals. We're undamaged. We're still okay."

"Are we? Are we not affected, forever changed by an event?"

"Depends on what the event is, Tam. When we were individually saved, we became new people in Christ. That's more important than anything, right?"

New people in Christ.

Ryan had memorized 2 Corinthians 5:17, but it wasn't the time and place for him to recite it to Tamsyn. He decided to keep it in his heart for later.

Therefore, if anyone is in Christ, he is a new creation; old things have passed away; behold, all things have become new.

"Yes." Tamsyn nodded. "Salvation is the biggest event of my life."

"So everything else pales in comparison. House fires, for example. Property damages, job losses, such things. *Things.*" Ryan paused to see if Tamsyn had anything else to add.

When she didn't, he continued. "And then there's our event."

"*Our* event?"

"When we met."

"I let you go."

"I'm still here, Tam. I'll always be here for you." Ryan stepped close enough to hold her hand. "We'll walk down this path together. We'll rebuild. Restore. Renovate. Reconstruct. Together."

"It won't be the same house." Tamsyn sniffled.

"It'll be better—because God is with us."

"Mom used to say that everything is going to be okay in the Lord."

"Wise words. God is all we need." Ryan hugged Tamsyn tightly, praying in his heart that she wouldn't turn him away again.

She didn't. She stayed there in his arms.

They said nothing for a while until the afternoon July sun beat down on them, and Ryan began to sweat.

Tamsyn pulled back and wiped sweat off her cheeks. "Your sweat is all over my face."

"It's hot out here. Whose bright idea was it to come here after lunch on a hot July afternoon?"

"Me. I had to see the place."

Ryan nodded. "Looks pretty bad. What are you going to do? Clean up?"

"Not yet. The insurance company is sending someone tomorrow when their office opens up. I asked my friend Sabine—she's a real estate agent and property manager—and she said my insurer is pretty good about paying for replacement in kind and trying to get original fixtures."

"That's wonderful, but it's going to be hard to find nineteenth-century antiques like that massive fireplace."

"Well, we have the entire house on DVD, thanks to you." Tamsyn reached for Ryan's cheek and kissed it lightly. "But I may not restore it exactly. I've never liked that awful fireplace. It came with the house. I think it's time to find something period authentic, but perhaps more cheerful."

Ryan laughed. "A cheerful Victorian home? Now that's a contradiction."

"Is it? You'd be surprised." Tamsyn waved her arms around. "I think it's time for a makeover. I never liked the yellow-and-brown exterior trim. I think I want teal and blue or something that reminds me of the ocean."

"A teal Victorian. Whew. At least you didn't say pink."

Tamsyn spun around. "What's wrong with pink?"

"I can't imagine living in a pink—"

Tamsyn's horrified look stopped Ryan. "You can't move in with me."

"I have the passkey." Ryan dug into his pocket. A small box appeared in his hand. He dropped to his knees.

Tamsyn gasped.

He couldn't get the box to open with his sweaty fingers. "They told me it wasn't a puzzle box."

Tamsyn chuckled as Ryan finally ripped the box apart at the hinges. A ring rolled out onto the grimy sidewalk. "Oops."

Ryan retrieved it. Wiped the mud off the ring, making a couple of streaks on his jeans.

He had picked up the ring at Jared's favorite

jeweler in downtown Savannah after he left the airport no more than a couple of hours before. The store was open the day after Independence Day, but the proprietor had the entire week off. Jared had insisted that Ryan talked with no one else but Eloise. A quick emergency phone call from Jared made her go to work just for Ryan. She had on a sarong and a pair of flip-flops, and her hair smelled of chlorine from a swimming pool, but it didn't bother Ryan one bit as long as she sold him a ring today.

And he didn't care how much it cost.

Ryan remembered Hiroki's words.

Can't fight love.

The diamond ring was a brand-new design and yet it looked like an old marquis ring.

"Here's my passkey to move in with you," Ryan said, lifting up the ring toward Tamsyn. "Tamsyn Rosa Pendegrast, will you or will you not marry me? Please don't turn me down a second time."

"Did you say passkey? We can't live together until we get married."

"I'll stay with your dad." Ryan knew he had surprised Tamsyn when he saw her face. "Yes, I'm moving to Savannah."

"Seriously?"

"RYUCP is expanding to the coast."

"I thought you were proposing," Tamsyn said.

"He was?"

The deep voice of Jerome Pendegrast blasted Ryan's ears.

"That's some clumsy proposal. Did you even find the ring you dropped?"

Ryan turned toward him to respond, but he clammed up when he saw the crowd around them. Not only was Jerome standing there, so were Pastor Flores and his wife and a passel of neighborhood kids, one of them holding a basketball.

Ryan recognized three of the teens as the ones who had prevented Tamsyn from going back to her house the night before. They had probably saved her from being burned.

"Miss Tam," one of the teens said. "Is this guy giving you any trouble?"

Tamsyn shook her head.

"You let us know, and we'll take care of him."

"Thank you, Hector." Tamsyn's eyes didn't leave Ryan.

Ryan thought she was positively smiling now.

"We want to be invited to the wedding," Hector added.

Another kid chimed in. "So maybe you could tell him *yes* so we can get back to our game."

"Let him speak," Hector told his friend. "You can see he's a bit slow."

Ryan swallowed. *All right. Take two.* "Marry me, please?"

"Why?" Tamsyn asked.

"I love you, not because of our historical moments together, or the lovely tea we had on your back porch, or the little cruise on the riverboat, or the memorable walking tours... I love you for who you are in Christ, for your desire to please God even at your own expense, for letting God shape your life even when it's difficult." Ryan shuffled forward on his knees.

Tamsyn stepped forward to meet him. She held his face in her hands.

"I'm totally miserable without you, and every time I'm with you, I see and remember the grace and mercy of God toward us," Ryan said. "I do love you. I love, love, love you."

Tamsyn grinned. "You're repeating yourself."

"I'm repeating history." Ryan was still on his knees. "Didn't your grandfather propose to your grandmother in this house?"

"In the sitting room."

"Close enough."

Tamsyn laughed.

"We'll rebuild this house for our children and their children," Ryan said. "Something old, something new. Do you love me, Tamsyn?"

"Yes."

"Marry me." *Please don't say no.*

"All right, I will."

"The word is..." He needed the confirmation.

"Yes, Ryan. I'll marry you."

Everyone cheered and clapped, Jerome the loudest of all.

Ryan slid the slightly muddy ring onto Tamsyn's finger. He got to his feet. She was smiling broadly, tears in her eyes. Ryan wiped away the tears on her cheeks, smearing a bit of mud on her face.

Uh-oh.

He was trying to wipe off that mud streak from Tamsyn's cheeks, when a wad of tissue paper appeared in front of him. He took it from Heidi's hand, nodding to her in appreciation.

His betrothed all cleaned up, Ryan caressed her lips with his thumb and then with his own lips.

CHAPTER TWENTY-THREE

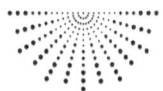

*E*leven months and a few days to spare.

That was how long it had taken Brooks Renovations to rebuild the destroyed Pendegrast residence and renovate it into the new Pendegrast-Ruttledge House.

Between Ryan and Tamsyn, they had scoured antique stores and online catalogs, commissioned pickers or crossed out wanted items, all in their attempt to refurnish the new home in the spirit of what had been, while still accommodating modern living and a bit of open-floor design wherever possible.

Tamsyn was glad that she and Ryan had left at least half the house empty. Perhaps their honeymoon in the Cotswolds would yield some lovely things they could add to their collection.

And no, it wasn't all old things. For Ryan's sake, they had incorporated new things, like that Sub-Zero refrigerator they both wanted so they could store enough food for entertaining friends from church and work. And the must-have Wi-Fi on every floor in the entire house.

Something old, something new.

Just the way they wanted it.

In an hour, Lord willing, they would be out of this riverboat wedding reception and on their way to their new home. Until then, Tamsyn searched for her dad to be sure he was all right.

He found her first. His jacket was off, revealing a bright Hawaiian shirt.

That's Dad.

"My lovely, lovely daughter. All grown up." Dad hugged Tamsyn so tightly she thought he might rip up the handmade lace on the antique wedding gown.

But it held up.

Just like a lot of things in their lives.

"Are you going to be okay for about four days?" Tamsyn asked between tears.

"Hey, don't worry about me. I'll be busy giving tours. I'm not sure if I'm going to get any downtime in four days."

Tamsyn nodded. Yes, it was the right move to ask Dad to cover for her at the office of Tamsyn

Tours. He wasn't going to do any walking tours due to his bad knees, but he could talk up a storm on those trolley tours.

Speaking of trolleys, she hoped their ride was on time.

It wasn't that she wasn't enjoying the reception. She had been on her toes in these four-inch heels long enough. She wished she had just worn flip-flops like some of her friends had done at their beach weddings.

But she had chosen to have her wedding here on the *Caleigh Pendegrast* riverboat in honor of Mom.

She will always be in my heart.

"I wish Mom were here," she said.

"Me too, Tam. Me too. But she's in heaven, and they're having a feast bigger than this. Someday we're going to go up there and party with her!"

Tamsyn laughed. "We will, Dad!"

"We will what?" Ryan came from behind Tamsyn and squeezed her waist.

"Party, Son. What else?" Dad toasted his new bridegroom again and waved to someone across the dining room. "Oh, I must go say hello to Gladys. Her husband, my Sunday School teacher, just passed. She'll need some support."

And Dad was off.

"You think your dad will date again?" Ryan asked as he locked his fingers in Tamsyn's, his wedding band pressing against her right-hand fingers.

"Maybe. I hope so."

Tamsyn glanced down at her left hand, at her rings. She remembered that smoldering day when Ryan proposed to her amid the ruins of her beloved home, how it had felt so right that it couldn't be wrong.

Like phoenixes, out of the ashes, a new day arose.

And yet, it wasn't mythology that sealed the moment for her. It was more than that.

Beyond houses and properties and things, beyond memories and legacies and ideas, Tamsyn had the certainty that, in Christ, everything would be all right regardless of what happened in her life and the lives of the Pendegrast family members— including Mom's cancer and death, Dad's widow-hood, and Tamsyn's loss of the family home.

We will rebuild.

Those were Ryan's words that day he had proposed to her.

"What did you think of my mother?" Ryan whispered in her ear. He looked in the general direction of the crowd where everyone seemed to be eating giant pieces of the wedding cake that Piper's pastry chef had baked for them.

"She's lovely. I've promised to have tea with her

and to go shopping with your grandmother when we're in the Cotswolds next week."

"And to meet all my relatives."

Tamsyn smiled. "I've always wanted to visit the English countryside."

Ryan's iPhone pinged. "Our ride is here. Let's go home, Mrs. Ruttledge."

Let's go home, Mrs. Ruttledge.

Ryan pulled her hand, and they wove through the crowd.

Everyone went outside the dining room, across the deck, down to the riverfront, and then up a ramp toward the awaiting Tamsyn Trolley parked on River Street, decked out in lace.

Tamsyn hugged Ryan's mom, then her relatives and friends. She found Piper Peyton at the end of the line nearest the trolley. Her bridesmaid was pretty in pink, but she was sobbing for some reason.

"Here's what you told me to hold for you," Piper signed.

"Thank you." Tamsyn didn't want to leave the gift from Ryan's mom with the rest of the wedding presents. Her new mother-in-law had brought it all the way from England, and Tamsyn wanted to see what was in it as soon as possible.

She had put Dad in charge of keeping the rest of the wedding gifts until after the honeymoon. It was easy; he would just ask his riverboat stewards to stash them in an empty cabin until Tamsyn picked them up after their trip to England.

Near the trolley, Ryan shook Hiroki Yamada's hand. The best man beamed with joy and then signed to Piper.

Oh boy. Tamsyn rolled her eyes. Hiroki had just asked Piper out on a date, and what did she say? She said *yes.*

Sigh!

Tamsyn boarded the trolley with Ryan and blew a kiss to Dad, who was standing next to a demure Gladys.

Uh-oh. What's Dad up to?

Ryan seemed to know what was on her mind.

"Don't worry about your dad," he said. "God is going to work out all things for his good."

CHAPTER TWENTY-FOUR

*a*s the trolley driver drove them straight toward Rosa Pendegrast Lane, Tamsyn thanked God for the air conditioner.

"Remind me again why we decided to marry in July?" But she already knew the answer.

"Because the house wasn't ready in April when the azaleas bloomed." Ryan eyed the wrapped gift on Tamsyn's lap. "Is that from my mother?"

Tamsyn nodded. She untied the lovely ribbons and loosened the sprig of silk flowers entwined in them. She carefully tore open the thick wrapping paper.

She gasped.

It was an old leather-bound Bible, its edges slightly worn.

She looked at Ryan, who only smiled.

Tamsyn read the card inside. "To my daughter-in-law. May God bless your marriage. From your mother-in-law and grandmother-in-law."

She chuckled. "A lot of 'in-laws' in there."

"That's my mother. She puts you in your place."

"I'm sure she means well." Tamsyn opened the Bible to the copyright page. "This Bible was printed in 1811."

"It's even older than your mom's lost Bible."

"The Word of God is never lost, Ryan." Tamsyn remembered one of the verses that Mom had loved to read to her from 1 Peter 1:24–25. She found the passage in her new Bible.

> *"All flesh is as grass,*
> *And all the glory of man as the flower of the*
> *grass.*
> *The grass withers,*
> *And its flower falls away,*
> *But the word of the Lord endures forever."*
> *Now this is the word which by the gospel was*
> *preached to you.*

"The word of God endures forever," Ryan echoed.

"Where do you think your mom found this Bible?"

"My guess is that she bought it at an antiquarian

bookstore in Cirencester. We'll ask her next week. I do know that she rarely goes anywhere anymore, though she made it to our wedding."

"I think I'm going to like your mom."

"Don't get too cozy. We're not moving to England, not after we've spent all year renovating our new family home."

"Savannah is our home," Tamsyn said.

"Hmmm." Ryan's fingers fiddled with the ringlets in Tamsyn's hair as the trolley navigated old Savannah squares where Tamsyn had conducted walking tours. "I enjoyed our tours. I remember walking on that sidewalk over there."

"You took every tour Tamsyn Tours offers. I wasn't sure what to expect when you hopped on the trolley for the first time for the Historic Homes Tour."

"And it was nice of you to give me free tour tickets for filling in for you at your office just before the Colonial Squares Tour. Remember that one? Your guide had stomach flu or something."

"Yeah, Mike did. I'm glad you were there and that you helped," Tamsyn said. "Much appreciated."

Ryan scooted closer to her on the bench seat. "When we come home from England, let's get on one of those Friday night couples' cruises. We'll do it right this time."

Tamsyn blushed.

"That too." Ryan held Tamsyn's hands in his.

Tamsyn felt his thumbs rubbing against her palms. Saying nothing more, he smiled into her eyes and pressed his forehead gently against hers like he had done the day they had tea on her back porch.

As if sensing she was waiting for it, Ryan reached for her lips, and Tamsyn knew they were his for a lifetime.

DEAR READER:

How was the romance between Tamsyn and Ryan? Hope you had fun touring the city of Savannah. I enjoyed writing *Walk You There* with its nod to area history. This story offers a glimpse of nineteenth century Georgia through the seasoned eyes of Tamsyn, our local tour guide and preservationist, as well as the new eyes of Ryan, the developer who comes to an understanding of history.

The next book in the Savannah Sweethearts series is *Love You Always*, the story of former FBI special agent Camden La Salle and his high school sweetheart, Iris Delaney. This book is a second chance romance novel with a dash of suspense. Happy reading!

Love You Always (Savannah Sweethearts Book 7)
JanThompson.com/love

NEW TO SAVANNAH SWEETHEARTS?

Are you new to the Savannah Sweethearts series? *Ask You Later* kicks off this series of clean and wholesome contemporary Christian romances set in Savannah and on Tybee Island by the Atlantic Ocean.

Ask You Later (Savannah Sweethearts Book 1)
JanThompson.com/ask

READ A FREE EBOOK!

Set in Georgia, South Carolina, and Tennessee, this Christian romance tells the story of art gallery archivist Sheryl Breckenridge and world-famous sculptor Winton Pace.

Time for Me (A Vacation Sweethearts Prequel)
JanThompson.com/time-free

JOIN MY BOOK NEWS MAILING LIST

Want to keep up with my writing schedule and get the latest book news from me? Sign up for my mailing list and read my newsletters for behind-the-scene information as well as to get free and discounted books.

Jan Thompson's Mailing List
JanThompson.com/newsletter

PLEASE WRITE A REVIEW

Thank you for reading *Walk You There*. If you'd like to leave a review, please follow the link below to see the retailers that carry this ebook.

Walk You There (Savannah Sweethearts Book 6)
JanThompson.com/walk

Continue reading for a preview of *Love You Always*...

THE NEXT BOOK IS LOVE YOU ALWAYS

SAVANNAH SWEETHEARTS BOOK 7

Three abandoned children...
Two erstwhile sweethearts...
One missing sister...
And zero problem?

After she kissed him and ran off eleven years ago, Camden never wanted to see her again. But Iris is back in town caring for her nieces and baby nephew, and she needs his help.

Will Camden let go of their past history to help Iris with her present crisis for the sake of the children's future well-being?

IRIS'S ISSUES...

When Iris Delaney's five-year-old niece calls her unexpectedly to say that her baby brother has run out of diapers, Iris freaks out and speeds to Savannah to find that her estranged sister, a single mother, has abandoned three kids under the age of six for who knows how long.

Desperate, Iris calls Ming Wei, one of her old friends still living in her hometown, to help her track down the runaway mother. After all, Ming owns Savannah River Investigations, which has been in the news.

To her surprise, Ming sends the last person she ever wants to see again...

CAMDEN'S CALL...

Former FBI agent and burned-out private investigator Camden La Salle is back in Savannah, and is in need of a job. Apparently, stocking grocery store shelves is beyond his pay grade.

Ming Wei has just the right job for him to ease back into his PI role. Happy to get a paycheck and healthcare, Camden discovers that the client he has to deal with is his ex-girlfriend.

Now he's mad at Ming for setting him up.

At first it's awkward between Camden and Iris, but as things worsen for her two nieces and a baby nephew, the two adults must set aside their differences to keep the children together and try to provide a somewhat normal life for them.

But how can anything be normal anymore for Camden and Iris with their entire past catching up to them?

Love You Always (Savannah Sweethearts Book 7):
JanThompson.com/love

Savannah Sweethearts:
JanThompson.com/sweethearts

For book news, sign up for Jan's mailing list:
JanThompson.com/newsletter

LOVE YOU ALWAYS CHAPTER 1
SNEAK PEEK

"We're not hungry," five-year-old Peggy said earnestly. "We had turkey and bacon."

Iris Delaney reached for the nearest chair behind her and sat down. The rattan chair creaked, and the armrest was sticky. "Turkey and bacon?"

Her niece nodded. "We shared it with Blue, but he doesn't mind."

"Blue?"

"The cat. He's not really blue," Peggy explained. "He's sort of brown."

The atmosphere swirled around Iris's head. Her heart pounded against her rib cage. "Y-you ate cat food?!"

Peggy shrugged. "Only when we ran out of Cheerios."

"When did you run out?"

"Two days ago, I think."

"Two days! How long has your mother—aargh!"

The scream lodged in Iris's throat.

How could Bianca do this?

How could she leave three kids—five and under —home alone?

Where had she gone?

Iris's head throbbed.

It had been a very long day. She had customer support problems from afternoon until evening at her workplace in Jacksonville. Her shift at the call center wasn't over until eleven o'clock in the evening, but when Peggy had called at nine, Iris's world exploded.

Somehow Iris's older sister, Bianca, had left Iris's number on speed dial on a cell phone in the little girl's possession. Somehow Peggy knew which contact entry said her name.

Auntie Ibis.

When Peggy said that Griffin had run out of diapers and she couldn't stop him from crying, Iris was furious.

A poor, helpless ten-month-old baby running out of diapers? No way.

When Peggy then said she didn't know where her mom was, Iris panicked. She hadn't expected Bianca to pull this sort of trick on her own kids, but she had threatened before to leave them with their fathers—if she could track them down.

Iris hadn't believed she'd carry through with it.

Where are you, Bianca?

Iris had left Savannah years ago and had moved to San Francisco. She had lived there for almost ten years until last year when Bianca had called her, saying that Dad had dementia. It wouldn't be long now before the two sisters lost their dad.

Six months ago, Iris had found a new job in Jacksonville, the closest place to Savannah she wished to be, yet within driving distance of Reidsville, Georgia, where Dad was serving life in prison. That way she could visit him more often in the psychiatric ward, and at the same time, go home far away enough to leave behind a past nightmare she'd rather not relive.

Now, a new crisis had emerged.

Two hours to the end of her shift, and her boss at the call center could not comprehend why she had to leave work and drive up to Savannah to see to the well-being of her two nieces and a baby nephew.

On the spot, Iris quit her job at the call center. She had lasted six months.

Still, she hadn't wanted to work on Wednesday nights, anyway. She would rather go to the midweek service at church, which she had been missing since three people had left the call center in recent months, and she and another worker had been filling in for them until their supervisor could hire new replacements.

She googled and found the phone number of the Savannah-Chatham Metropolitan Police Department. She reported her sister as missing and pleaded for them to send someone to check on the three kids. She had their home address from last year when she had sent them some Christmas presents.

She floored the gas pedal all the way up interstate 95 to Tybee Island, arriving around eleven at night, and having even picked up diapers, coffee, frozen hot dogs, and whole wheat buns at a convenience store on the way. She didn't know how she managed to make that short grocery list, but there it was.

While speeding on the highway in her beat-up old car, she called the SCMPD again, and they confirmed that a patrol officer had been dispatched to the house.

Iris prayed like she had never done before, and somewhere between the exits to St. Simon's Island and Savannah, a couple of high school friends' names popped into her head. She instructed her smartphone to look up some of these names while she drove.

Ming Wei was the first name her phone read aloud to her. It sounded like he ran a private investigation firm. Perfect! She called him.

Ming didn't mind that she had woken him up. He assured her that she had done the right thing to call 911.

Next thing she knew, it was eleven at night, and she was pulling up on Bianca's driveway between two parked SCMPD patrol cars.

And there they were, her welcoming party.

Two disheveled and sleepy-looking kids standing at the door, flanked by a police officer.

Iris parked her car, took a deep breath, ran up to her greeters, and all was well—

Not!

When she entered her sister's house, she found that the entire interior was in a disarray. It was filthy and grimy and looked like a landfill. The whole place smelled bad.

Iris didn't bother to take off her shoes, and

wished she had boots on so she didn't step on what looked like rancid food stuck to the living room carpet.

A couple of windows in the living room were opened to let the outside air ventilate the place, but the horrid stench remained. Iris had never smelled anything like it.

She wondered what Bianca had been doing in this place.

Iris knew that as soon as the officers left, she would have to shut those windows. She was unfamiliar with this neighborhood, and she had three little kids to protect.

Well, right now the kids needed protection from themselves. A five-year-old had run the roost for at least two days, calling all the shots. Somehow they had managed to survive without their mother.

Have they fended for themselves before?

The possibility bothered Iris.

The patrol officer explained that what Iris saw had been how they had found the house. There were no other adults.

Yes, the children had been on their own for who knew how long.

Iris was glad she lived in Jacksonville now. It would have been worse had she still been in San Francisco. The flight alone, considering airport stopovers, would have taken well over seven hours.

Now that she—Bianca's only living relative not incarcerated—had arrived, the patrol officer said they could interview the children. Unfortunately, Peggy and Sibley were too sleepy to talk.

"I put the baby in his crib," Officer Garcia said, holding a ziplock bag containing a disposable phone that Peggy had used to call Iris only a few hours ago.

The other officer had already walked out of the front door.

"Thank you." Iris meant it.

"Detective Zimmerman will call tomorrow morning to follow up. Lock all your doors and windows."

"Is it safe for us to be here?"

"We walked through the house and found no signs of break-ins." Officer Garcia smiled. "Call 911 and we'll be right back."

That's comforting.

Yet Iris knew that only God could keep her and the three kids truly safe.

And Bianca too.

But one thing Iris knew for sure: she wasn't going to sleep tonight.

After the officers had left, Iris was alone with the three lost children of Tybee Island.

She checked on Griffin, who had dutifully fallen asleep again.

And now to feed the older two.

Iris stared at Peggy, who stared back at her with determined eyes, eyes that reminded Iris of...

Mom.

Peggy had her grandmother's eyes.

"Are you sure you're not hungry?" Iris asked again as she realized that she had left the hot dogs and buns somewhere next to Griffin's diapers when she had first arrived. "I can make some hot dogs. Don't you like hot dogs?"

"Only if it's kosher," Peggy said.

"But you're not Jewish."

"Mommy said we try to eat healthy."

"Cat food is not—aargh!"

Peggy stepped toward Iris, who was still sitting down. "Don't worry, Auntie Ibis. Pink likes turkey too."

"Pink? Pink?" Iris began hyperventilating.

Peggy sighed loudly. "Auntie Ibis, stop repeating your questions. I can hear you just fine."

"Tell. Me. Who. Pink. Is."

"A girl cat, of course. She's come to live with us."

"Since when?"

Peggy pointed to a wooden door that had scratches on it. "We found her in the backyard chasing a mouse, but she did it to feed her babies."

"Did you say babies? Baby what?"

Peggy tipped her head to one side, the same way

Iris's sister had done. There was so much of Bianca in her daughter.

Where is Bianca?

"Oh, you mean kittens?" Iris widened her eyes. "Baby cats?"

Peggy shook her head. "Everybody knows that kittens are baby cats."

"I know, but...but..."

Peggy's lips trembled. "Please don't send Pink away. She only has five babies left. We couldn't find the sixth baby. Sibby thinks the pelicans took it."

Sibley is three. What does a three-year-old know about life and death?

My poor, poor nieces and nephew.

"Pelicans don't eat kittens," Iris said, calming down.

"That's what I said. They prefer seafood." Peggy reached over and patted Iris's arm with her grimy, sticky hands. "See, Auntie Ibis. If you don't repeat your words, we can have a normal conversation."

Love You Always (Savannah Sweethearts Book 7): JanThompson.com/love

More Information about Savannah Sweethearts:
JanThompson.com/savannah

To keep up with Jan Thompson's book news:
JanThompson.com/newsletter

LOVE YOU ALWAYS CHAPTER 2 SNEAK PEEK

"Awkward! I can't see her, Ming." Camden La Salle folded his arms tightly around his chest, his boots tapping fiercely on the carpeted floor of his friend's office.

The Savannah morning sun shone through the wall of office windows, casting a spotlight on his face. He felt blindsided.

How could Ming do this?

"I didn't come home to this," Camden protested.

"This what? You need a job. I have an assignment. It pays well." Ming smiled.

Is that a knowing smile?

Camden frowned. "Of all the clients you have in the world, it has to be her."

"Why not?" Ming eased away from his old office chair that looked like another find from the local thrift shops.

In fact, the entire office was probably furnished from local secondhand finds, Camden thought, but that wasn't the point of this morning's discourse.

"Why can't you see her?" Ming asked again.

"Um, well, she...um—"

"Vetoed!" Ming laughed.

"Vetoed?" Camden scratched his head. "What?"

"Listen, I was just as surprised to hear from her in the middle of the night," Ming explained. "We haven't spoken in—what?—eleven years? Since you two broke up anyway. Whatever it is, she needs our help now. I'm busy with all these new assignments that Helen is dishing out to me. Besides, Sabine's on bed rest. I have to watch junior until our new baby arrives."

Camden didn't know what to say.

On the one hand, he wanted to help Ming. How

could he not? Ming had stood by him through thick and thin. Even when the FBI had fired him for insubordination—whatever!—Ming had not abandoned him.

They went a long way back. All the way to high school.

Same as with her.

Iris had been eighteen, had finished her senior year at Savannah High, and had started her freshman year at the same college Camden was in.

Camden had graduated from the same high school four years before but had to work for two years to earn enough income to go to college. When he finally made it to his freshman year, he met Iris at their weekly gun club meetings at the student center on campus.

"If you must know, I'm the first guy she kissed," Camden said quietly.

"The only people who didn't know that were Iris's parents."

"Yeah. They didn't like me because I wasn't saved then..."

"We all didn't like you, Cam."

"So there you have it. That's why we broke up her second year in college when she transferred out of state." Camden didn't want to relive it, but it had to be explained to Ming so that he could get out of this assignment.

True, they had only dated for one year, but Camden had always thought they had been serious enough to consider marriage.

"You and I know there's more to it than that. So it has been how many years now, and you're still hung up about her?"

"She'll remember me. Us."

Ming shrugged. "In any case, she's in a bad situation right now. The SCMPD is on it. All I'm asking you to do is organize a community search. Is that too much to ask?"

"There's no way you're putting me on the payroll for that."

"We'll sort that out later. Right now, keep your eyes and ears open. Something's afoot."

"Something's afoot?" Camden had to laugh. "You watching kiddie cartoons with your toddler again?"

Ming shrugged. "Everyone knows there's no way a mother with three young children would just up and leave, you know."

"Right."

"I think the least we can do is to organize the community to help us find Bianca—whatever we can that doesn't get in the way of police investigations. That's our cover story."

Camden groaned. Ming had suspected there

was more to Bianca's situation, and now Camden had to do the leg work.

"Besides, you could catch up," Ming said.

"I don't—"

"Iris is alone, stuck with three little kids. She has been away too long. Most of the people she knew no longer live here, except us. I think she knows Tamsyn since we all go way back to Savannah High. Maybe Mrs. Untermeyer. But not anyone else at church. Say, you could invite her to church."

Camden didn't move.

"Don't let your personal beef get in the way of ministry. She needs our help."

"You never forget your first kiss, Ming," Camden finally said.

"Sure you can. I did. When I married Sabine, I forgot and forsook everyone else." Ming swiped his iPhone. "I just forwarded you the transcript of our phone convo. Address and phone number are on there. Keep your emotions out of the interview. Get it done. Get out. As soon as I wrap up this job with Helen—I'm thinking by next Friday—I'll take over, if there's anything to be done. Does that sound good?"

Camden thought about it.

"One week?" he asked.

"Yeah. Get enough info for me to follow up later."

"And you're paying me."

"By the hour, as agreed. In a few months, I should be able to afford to hire a couple more investigators, and then you're free to go wherever you want. If you want to work for me, old friend, you just need to take the assignments I give you. That's how I keep the doors open for business."

Camden drew a deep breath. He needed this job. He had been out of work for a while, and no law enforcement agency would touch him after that fiasco four years ago. It had been a personal tragedy for him too, didn't they know? Losing his last girlfriend, Daljeet, in that botched operation had been on his mind month after month.

He had taken a hiatus in Ohio—as far away as he could go—for a couple of years, working night shifts, taking part-time security work, and living out of a rented trailer as he tried to hide from the world.

Prayers and constant communication from Diego Flores, his pastor at Riverside Chapel, and Ming Wei, his best friend in all the world apart from Jesus, had pulled him back into reality.

And then two weeks ago, Ming offered him a job at his Savannah River Investigations firm.

Here he was, back in Savannah, ready to start over.

Only he hadn't realized how it could open up old wounds.

And yet...

Camden sighed. He couldn't live off his credit cards. He couldn't sleep on other people's couches and backroom porches anymore. The next stop for him was a cardboard box under a bridge—if he could find an available bridge in Savannah.

He needed this job.

He needed to get back on track.

Swallowing his pride and past hurts, Camden mustered up whatever courage he had lost when Daljeet died, and he buried his face in his calloused hands.

"All right," he bit out. "Sorry about my rant."

Ming came around the desk and placed his hand on Camden's shoulder.

"I will always be your friend, no matter what you say to me," Ming said. "I know what you've been through, and I don't wish to walk in your shoes. I'm sorry that your first assignment at SRI dredges up a past you don't want to revisit."

Camden grunted.

"Unfortunately, if all we end up doing for Iris is organize a community search, I'm not getting paid, though I will still cut a paycheck for you."

"Understood." Camden nodded slowly. "I'll do it off hours if that's the case."

Why on earth did I say that?

"That's the attitude, Cam. Sometimes God

works in ways we cannot see, and this could be one of those times." Ming walked back to his chair. "Let's keep it professional, and I'll do my best to get her off your hands as soon as I can. Okay?"

Love You Always (Savannah Sweethearts Book 7):
JanThompson.com/love

More Information about Savannah Sweethearts:
JanThompson.com/savannah

To keep up with Jan Thompson's book news:
JanThompson.com/newsletter

READ A FREE EBOOK IN THE SAME STORY WORLD

Set in Georgia, South Carolina, and Tennessee, this clean and wholesome Christian romance tells the story of art gallery archivist Sheryl Breckenridge and world-famous sculptor Winton Pace. Read this ebook for free!

Time for Me (A Vacation Sweethearts Prequel)

JanThompson.com/time-free

ACKNOWLEDGMENTS

Many thanks to my Georgia Press publishing team for keeping up with my writing schedule.

I appreciate author Heather Day Gilbert for copyediting this book, and copyeditor Dori Harrell and proofreader Lenda Selph for proofreading it. Thank you, ladies!

I am grateful to God for my husband and son for their support and encouragement. I also thank God for my parents and my three brothers for my happy and memorable childhood. I'll always remember my beloved mother and my late father for having instilled in me the love of reading and writing from a very early age. I miss my father here on earth, but I will see him again in heaven someday.

Most of all, I am eternally thankful to my Lord and Savior, Jesus Christ, who died on the cross to save me from my sins and rose again from the grave to give me eternal life. Without Him, I can write nothing (John 15:5).

Jan Thompson
John 3:16

AUTHOR'S NOTE

OLD TOWN SAVANNAH

I remember walking on the deck of the *Bounty* when it docked in Savannah—only months before it was lost at sea in a storm that took lives, sadly. I also had some recollections of touring the USG *Eagle*. Lovely ships, both. Having said that, I must add that my own tall ships are based on my own imagination and have no bearings on existing ships. In other words, my own tall ships don't exist in real life.

I'm glad that most Savannah is preserved, though the fire at the end of the nineteenth century didn't help. However, some buildings have been reconstructed, so that's a good thing. The Trustees' Garden is still there—somewhat, like a green patch of grass—so there's that from the 1730s.

Someday, I will finish a historical series set in Savannah that I've been researching for years.

When my research is done—there are more first-person journals to read through—I will complete writing that series. It goes from the colonial era through the Civil War, and the main characters are the ancestors of some of the present-day characters in both my Seaside Chapel and Savannah Sweethearts series.

Happy reading!
Jan Thompson

BOOKS BY JAN THOMPSON

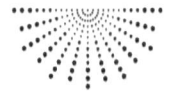

CONTEMPORARY CHRISTIAN CITY, COASTAL, AND BEACH ROMANCE

Seaside Chapel (7 Books)
JanThompson.com/seaside
Savannah Sweethearts (12 Books)
JanThompson.com/savannah
Vacation Sweethearts (8 Books)
JanThompson.com/vacation

CHRISTIAN ROMANTIC SUSPENSE AND NEAR-FUTURE TECHNOTHRILLERS

Protector Sweethearts (6 Books)

JanThompson.com/protector
Defender Sweethearts (6 Books)
JanThompson.com/defender
Binary Hackers (4 Books)
JanThompson.com/binary

SEASIDE CHAPEL

Welcome to *USA Today* bestselling author Jan Thompson's Seaside Chapel Christian beach romance series. These novels are set on real-life St. Simon's Island, Georgia—a beach town where history is all around and the future is a moment away—and the neighboring fictitious Seaside Island, where the rich and famous live.

Savor the small-town atmosphere and the warm southern beaches of St. Simon's Island and the idyllic Golden Isles along the Atlantic Ocean. Enjoy the music of the orchestra and hymns of the church, and hang out with our Christian friends who attend Seaside Chapel, a little church by the sea known for its beach weddings and fair share of love and life.

As these Christians grow in their knowledge and understanding of God, they are tested in their spiritual maturity, their love lives, and their relationships with others. Share their heartaches and healing, and cheer them on as they celebrate faith, family, and friends.

- Book 0 (Prequel): *His Surprise Proposal*
- Book 1: *His Longing Heart*
- Book 2: *His Wake-Up Call*
- Book 3: *His Morning Kiss*
- Book 4: *His Quiet Serenade*
- Book 5: *His Waiting Love*
- Book 6: *His Beach Retreat*

For more information about Seaside Chapel:
JanThompson.com/seaside

SAVANNAH SWEETHEARTS

Welcome to the new south! From *USA Today* bestselling author Jan Thompson come these clean and wholesome, sweet and inspirational Christian romances set on the romantic beaches of Tybee Island and in the coastal town of Savannah, Georgia. Meet a group of multiracial and multiethnic churchgoing Christians who love the Lord, work hard in their careers, and seek God's will for their love lives. Against a backdrop of ocean, sand, and sun, these inspirational romances showcase aspects of the human need for God and for one another. Have some tea, settle in a comfortable reading chair, and enjoy these sweet celebrations of faith, hope, and love in Jesus Christ.

- Book 1: *Ask You Later* (Artist Romance)

- Book 2: *Know You More* (Multiracial Romance)
- Book 3: *Tell You Soon* (Asian-American Romance with Suspense)
- Book 4: *Draw You Near* (International Romance)
- Book 5: *Cherish You So* (Wheelchair Billionaire Romance)
- Book 6: *Walk You There* (Old-Meets-New Tour Guide Romance)
- Book 7: *Love You Always* (Romance with Suspense)
- Book 8: *Kiss You Now* (Multiracial Romance)
- Book 9: *Find You Again* (Multiracial Romance)
- Book 10: *Wish You Joy* (Christmas-Themed Romance)
- Book 11: *Call You Home* (Deaf Chef Romance)
- Book 12: *Let You Go* (Asian-American Romance with Suspense)

For more information about Savannah Sweethearts:
JanThompson.com/savannah

VACATION SWEETHEARTS

Travel with our friends from Savannah, Georgia, to the coast and to the mountains. Cheer them on as they celebrate the immeasurable grace and undeserved mercy of God through Jesus Christ.

The Vacation Sweethearts novels are a spin-off of Jan's Savannah Sweethearts series, and fans will recognize familiar faces from Riverside Chapel, a church in the coastal city of Savannah, Georgia. In fact, we might even visit the beach town of Tybee Island from time to time to visit old friends and beloved families...

- Book o (Prequel): *Time for Me*
- Book 1: *Smile for Me* (International Romance)

- Book 2: *Reach for Me* (Romance with Suspense)
- Book 3: *Wait for Me* (Romance with Suspense)
- Book 4: *Look for Me* (Romance with Suspense)
- Book 5: *Pray for Me* (International Romance)
- Book 6: *Care for Me* (Small Mountain Town Romance)
- Book 7: *Cheer for Me* (International Romance)

Read *Time for Me* (Prequel) for free:
JanThompson.com/time-free

For more information about Vacation Sweethearts:
JanThompson.com/vacation

PROTECTOR SWEETHEARTS

Private investigator Helen Hu and her associates specialize in searching for missing persons and hunting for lost treasures. Join them in their adventure suspense around the world in *USA Today* best-selling author Jan Thompson's Protector Sweethearts, a series of Christian Romantic Suspense with a side of mystery.

Protector Sweethearts is a spin-off of Savannah Sweethearts and Vacation Sweethearts.

- Book 1: *Once a Thief*
- Book 2: *Once a Hero*
- Book 3: *Once a Spy*
- Book 4: *Twice a Fighter*
- Book 5: *Twice a Convict*
- Book 6: *Twice a Soldier*

For more information about Protector Sweethearts:
JanThompson.com/protector

DEFENDER SWEETHEARTS

Defender Sweethearts is a sister series to the Protector Sweethearts Christian romantic suspense collection. While the heroes in Protector Sweethearts search for lost treasures and lost people, the Defender Sweethearts novels focus on protecting the helpless and hopeless. The main characters in Defender Sweethearts come from the supporting cast in Protector Sweethearts.

- Book 1: *Never a Traitor*
- Book 2: *Never a Hostage*
- Book 3: *Never a Fugitive*
- Book 4: *Always a Maverick*
- Book 5: *Always a Champion*
- Book 6: *Always a Guardian*

For more information about Defender Sweethearts:
JanThompson.com/defender

BINARY HACKERS

Like more suspense with your Christian romance? Like to read suspense thrillers? If you're looking for clean near-future romantic suspense without compromising the Christian faith, these books are for you.

From *USA Today* bestselling author Jan Thompson come these inspirational near-future cyberthrillers combining technothriller and romance, starting with Binary Hackers that feature computer specialists living at the edge of cyberspace, where they have to juggle being law-abiding truth-telling Christians while carrying out their assignments by any and all means possible.

The Binary Hackers series is set in the same story world as Jan's other books, and characters from the other series may make cameo appearances in this series and vice versa.

- Book 1: *Zero Sum*
- Book 2: *Zero Day*
- Book 3: *Zero Base*
- Book 4: *Zero Trust*

For more information about Binary Hackers:
JanThompson.com/binary

ABOUT JAN THOMPSON

USA Today bestselling author Jan Thompson writes clean and wholesome contemporary Christian romance with elements of women's fiction, Christian romantic suspense with an air of mystery, and inspirational international thrillers with threads of sweet Christian romance. Jan's books are for readers who love inspiring stories of faith, hope, and love in Jesus Christ.

Raised on a tropical island in the eastern hemisphere, Jan now lives and writes in the western hemisphere. Her international background gives her a unique multicultural and multiracial perspective to her novels and books. The island has never left her, and she reminisces about beach life in her beach romance novels.

When Jan is not busy writing small-town stories, she writes big-city romantic suspense and international technothrillers, a nod to her previous career in computer science. She weaves technology with human interests, reflecting the current and future digital world. And romance. There's always romance.

Beyond the printed page, Jan is a wife, mother, family scribe, avid reader, occasional artist, erstwhile pianist, and chief of staff to the family cat.

Find out more about Jan Thompson:
JanThompson.com

Subscribe to Jan's book news mailing list:
JanThompson.com/newsletter

For God so loved the world
that He gave His only begotten Son,
that whoever believes in Him
should not perish
but have everlasting life.
—John 3:16